Copyright Page
The Draoidh's Accord

© [2026] [Joseph L Wiess]

For permission requests, write to the publisher at:
[Golden Plains Press]

[JosephWiess@gmail.com]

ISBN: [979-8-9934166-7-0]

Cover Design: [Joseph L Wiess]

Printed in the United States of America

To Bill, Dave, Kathrine, and Black Knight. You're
the best.

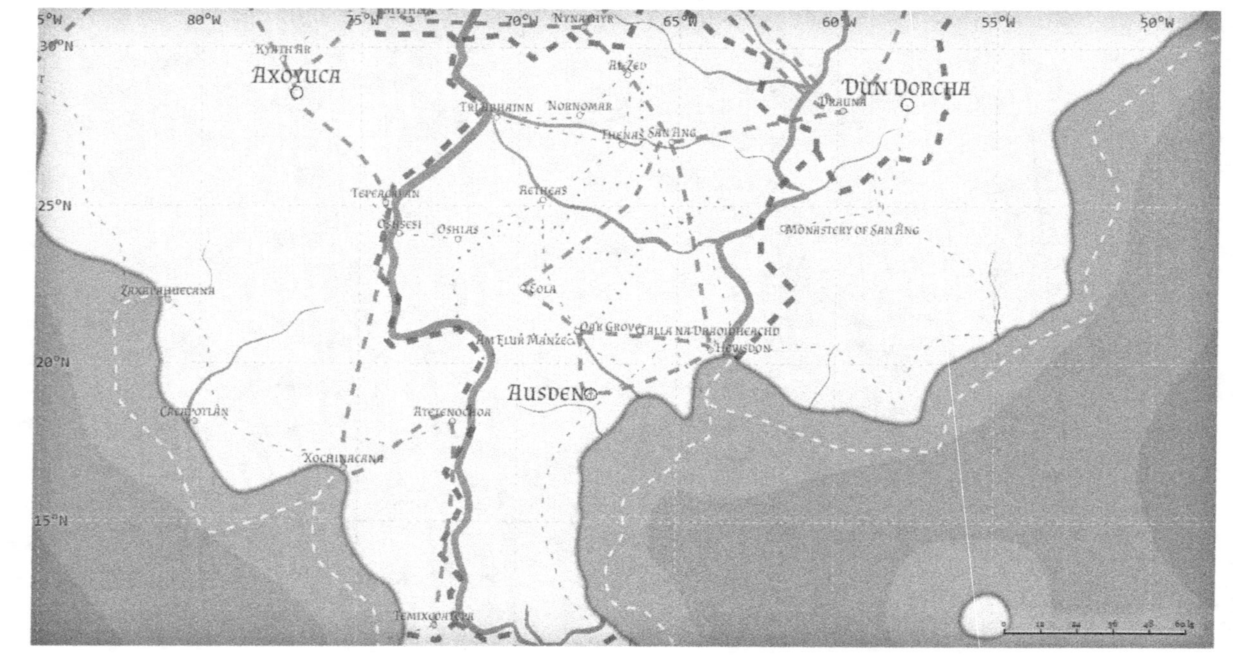

85°W
80°W
75°W
70°W
NYNATHYR
65°W
60°W
55°W
50°W
30°N
25°N
20°N
15°N
AXOYUCA
KYNTHÁR
DÙN DORCHA
DRAUNA
ALZED
TRIABHAINN
NORNOMAR
THENAS SAN ÄNG
RETHEAS
TEPEACHAN
CSASESI
OSHIAS
ZAXALAHUECANA
EOLA
MONASTERY OF SAN ÄNG
OAK GROVE
TALLA NA DRAOIDHEACHD
HEUSDON
AM ELUR MANZEC
AUSDEN
ATETENOCHOA
CACHPOTLÁN
XOCHINACANA
TEMIXCOATEPA
0 12 24 36 48 60 k

Contents

Chapter One

Of Bonds and Thrones

Ria blinked and shook her head as the shadows opened up, and she found herself standing across the oasis from her people's manor house. The sudden stillness pressed against her ears, the murmur of magic fading like a sigh. The air smelled faintly of wet stone and desert bloom, the mingled fragrance of lilies and night-warmed reeds. Moonlight rippled across the water's surface, and faint waves lapped against the bank, stirred by a whispering wind that smelled of salt and sand.

She gazed across the oasis, wondering why she had come out so far from the house. The manor shimmered in the distance, its pale stone walls softened by the lanterns that burned near the gates.

She had pictured arriving in the back garden, beneath the vine-draped balcony of her childhood rooms, not on the pond's edge beneath the open stars.

"Oh well," she whispered, picking up her skirt and stepping further onto the pond's bank. The grass, cool and damp beneath her feet, clung to her shoes as if reluctant to let her go. She breathed deeply, filling her lungs with the sweet scent of the lilies in bloom, and smiled as she set her eyes on the manor house and started in that direction. Her eyes caught the distant light, more than most would, and the path gleamed faintly before her like a thread of silver.

It took her almost half an hour to circle the pond and pick up the path leading to the front gate in the wooden fence surrounding the grounds.

The night was thick with the hum of insects, the chirping of frogs, and the low rustle of the palms leaning over the water. Her heartbeat kept time with her steps, a soft, steady rhythm echoing the strange certainty that she was coming home for the last time, **because she knew she would never belong here again** .

"Stay where you are and make no move."

Ria stopped at once. The command cut through the still air, followed by the sound of bowstring drawn taut. A glint of light on metal brought her gaze to the guard who stood beyond the gate, his longbow raised, the arrow's head catching a shard of moonlight.

When she complied, another voice came from her left side. "Who are you, and why are you here?" She recognized the tone, measured, wary, and edged with authority, the voice of the guard's lieutenant.

With a nod, Ria dipped her head in acquiescence. "Good evening, Lieutenant Bal-Shazar," she said with a certain amount of humor. "I know I've been gone for a while, but you should still recognize me."

The lieutenant looked suspicious as he walked around her. His boots crunched softly over gravel; the faint scent of oiled leather and steel drifted past her. "Your Grace," he said in a monotone as he recognized her. "The last message we received put you on the skyship of the Darkblades." His eyes searched her face, noticing something that nagged at him. "Where did you come from?"

Ria closed her eyes, feeling his gaze upon her like a tangible weight. "I come from Am Flur Manse, Mac Draoidheachd's home," she whispered.

A stern expression crossed his face, and he frowned. "You will follow me, not deviate from our path, and explain yourself to General Makar."

"As you wish, Lieutenant Bal-Shazar," she replied as she followed him through the gate and up the path to the front door of the manor house.

The air grew warmer as they walked beneath the shadow of the outer walls. The familiar scent of cedar and rose oil reached her, lingering from the lamps that burned by the entrance. Every sound, the scrape of a hinge, the tread of armored boots on stone, felt sharper than she remembered, as though her senses, honed by shadow travel, caught every vibration of her old home's heartbeat.

Once inside, she waited in the foyer that once belonged to her.

The marble floor reflected the torchlight in long, golden lines, and the scent of beeswax polish mingled with the faint perfume of desert myrrh. Portraits of her ancestors stared down from the walls, their painted eyes seeming to follow her, judging, questioning, remembering. The lieutenant sent a servant to find the General.

Within minutes, the General joined the two, who, like the lieutenant, circled Ria as he examined her. The steady rhythm of his boots on stone was the only sound between them.

Ria had the sudden, uneasy sense that the General already knew what the lieutenant had only begun to suspect.

"Ilyriatri, where have you been, and to whom have you bonded?"

She knew that if anyone could figure it out, it would be the General.

Ria gave him a half-bow. "As I told Lieutenant Bal-Shazar, I have come from Am Flur Manse."

Makar's eyes widened slightly as she named where she had been. "Mac Draoidheachd—Rhyslin Darkblade has sent me to invite you to his house so that he can discuss the treaty I mentioned in my letter."

Silence followed her answer. The older general did not speak at once, and the pause stretched long enough for Ria to feel the weight of it settle in her chest.

Torchlight flickered across his face, deepening the lines etched into his brow as he studied her.

At last, he drew a measured breath. "To whom did you bond?"

Ria blushed slightly, her gaze dropping to the marble at her feet before lifting again to meet his. "I am an dara bhanna to Rhyslin Darkblade, Mac na draoidheachd, mac uchd-mhacachd na Màthar."

Makar regarded her for a long moment, his expression unreadable. Then he inclined his head. "Might I ask why?"

Ria searched for an answer he would accept. She could not bring herself to say that it had begun in selfishness, in fear of what awaited her if she remained alone. When no easy explanation came, she said softly, "I thought he might be Ciad-Fhir."

At that, his brow lifted a fraction. The Ciad-Fhir were almost a myth. The First men to set foot on Crann Na Beatha. The one's rumored to guard Astinmah's forest retreat.

Rhyslin Darkblade may be old, but he's not that old."

"I realize that," Ria said. "Then I fell in love with him." She held her breath, bracing herself for the rebuke she was certain would follow.

Instead, he only watched her, something thoughtful settling into his gaze. "If I were to ask him, what would he say?"

She looked up into his eyes. "He would say that I submitted myself to him, willingly, and begged him for his bond."

"Ilyriatri," he muttered. "You realize that being bound to him means you are no longer Queen."

The truth of it struck with familiar force. Love and longing welled in her chest, and she did not try to hide them. From the way his gaze lingered on her face, she knew he saw it.

"Yes," he said quietly. "You do realize that."

His posture shifted then, subtle, but unmistakable, as if a final piece had fallen into place. When he spoke again, his voice was steady. "I see. You came to abdicate your position."

Ria nodded.

He released a slow breath. "What would you have of us, Ilyriatri?"

"Take control of the council and sign the treaty," she whispered. "It is what is best for our people."

"What does he call you?"

Ria licked her lips. "He calls me Ria." She reached out, daring to rest her hand against his arm. "I love him, Makar. I haven't felt that since Garion died."

The years seemed to settle more heavily upon him then. He covered her hand with his own. "I see. I could never deny you anything, Ria. I hope you find happiness." His sigh echoed faintly against the high ceiling. "Of course, I'll sign the treaty. Our people need hope."

Another blush crept across her face. "Rhyslin said you'd have a way to get us to Am Flur Manse. Maighstir Darkblade has extended an invitation to stay with him and said the council is meeting in seven days."

Makar released her hand and ran his fingers through his hair. "I'll only need a few uarian to get ready. Rhyslin was right. A' Mathair will transport us to Mac Draoidheachd's home." He blew out a slow breath, then addressed the lieutenant. "Show Ria into the sitting room. I'll be back in an uair."

"Yes, sir," the officer replied as the General turned and left the room.

The door closed softly behind him, leaving Ria alone with the faint echo of his boots and the steady flicker of the torches.

She exhaled, her heart steady but heavy, and for the first time since stepping through the shadows, she allowed herself to feel what she had given up—and what she had gained.

As the shadow enveloped her, the golden-haired princess turned bhanna closed her eyes, drawing in a trembling breath.

The air around her was neither warm nor cold, an in-between place, dense and soundless. Her heartbeat thudded in her ears like distant drums, the only rhythm she could hold onto.

She thought very hard about her mother. Imagining Allanagh without tying her to a place or time was the hardest thing she had ever done. In her mind, faces and moments collided: the mother who sang by firelight when Flur was small; the queen on the battlements at Three Rivers Fort; the woman standing beside her when she gave her bond to Rhyslin. She tried to think of the essence of her mother, the scent of her hair, the strength of her embrace, the light in her eyes—but each time, her mind slipped back into images of walls and rooms, of castles and forests.

The shadows seemed to sense her confusion. They thickened and stirred, their roiling depths folding like ink in water. The nothingness around her shivered, tugging her toward places long gone: the stone corridors of Green Mountain Castle, the worn wooden steps of their cottage deep in the forest.

Flur huffed in frustration and sank to her knees. The ground beneath her palms was neither earth nor air, soft as smoke, yet solid enough to hold her. She pressed her hands to her face, despair flickering in her chest.

"Màthair, tha feum agam ort. Càite a bheil thu?" she whispered, her voice trembling. The words fell into the dark like stones into deep water.

For a long moment, nothing answered. Then the shadows began to whisper back.

"Why are you giving up, little one? Why don't you give up and let us take you?"

The voices were soft at first, childlike and coaxing. Then they multiplied, overlapping, hungry, cruel, and ancient. Their murmurs twisted through her hair like cold fingers. Panic surged through her chest, and she clapped her hands over her ears, shaking her head.

"Mathair!" she screamed, and her cry broke the stillness like glass.

In that instant, the whispers recoiled.

The dark shuddered, and through the blackness came a burst of memory so vivid it blinded her: her mother's face, her smile, her voice.

Light erupted, faint, golden, and warm.

Flur found herself standing on solid ground once more. A circle of weathered stones surrounded her, each one etched with spiraling runes that glowed faintly as if lit from within.

The air smelled of moss and cold iron, and the faint sound of wind whispered through grass. Before her stood a tomb, ancient, solemn, and vaguely familiar.

For a long while, she simply stared. Her heart pounded as she tried to place the site, but the memory eluded her. Even the stars above seemed strange. With careful steps, she approached the tomb.

The structure was built of pale marble veined with green, its understated columns worn smooth by time. Vines crept up from the base, climbing toward the lintel where they intertwined above the archway like clasped hands. Moonlight pooled across the carvings, and Flur's eyes followed the lines of the vines upward, her fingertips brushing the cool stone.

Unbidden, tears welled in her eyes. She could feel the stillness of this place—the deep hush of reverence, the weight of old love. Taking another step forward, she let her gaze fall on the inscription carved into the double doors.

"Four tribes, once bound, now torn by strife,

Jealous hearts that shattered life.

Yet three arose, in love made whole,

Children of the mounts, where doves silvered soar,

Children of the woods, where ancient trees stand tall,

Children of the sands, where shifting dunes call.

One king to bind, to heal, to guide,

Four as one, standing side by side.

Here rests the King, the firstborn's light,

Garion, son of Alorn, in endless night."

As she read the lines of the first language, understanding flooded her, and she gasped. Her knees buckled, and she fell before the door, tears spilling freely.

"Papa, oh Papa," she wept, not for herself but for all that had been lost. Her voice cracked softly as she whispered, "Rana would have loved you. You would have loved Rana, Papa. She's a lot like you."

Her hand trembled as she traced the final rune, the one that would open the doors.

A soft voice echoed from within, muffled but alert. "Who's there?"

The doors swung open on silent hinges, gliding like shadows themselves.

Flur slipped inside, her steps light as mist. The air was cool and still, heavy with the scent of ancient stone and faded incense. Her fingers brushed the carved walls as she passed, and her tears continued to fall, unchecked, endless.

The silence of the tomb pressed close, broken only by her faint breathing and the soft pad of her feet.

She remembered this feeling, the tremulous awe that had seized her when she first met Rhyslin, when she had offered herself to him. It was the same surrender of spirit, the same ache of reverence.

When she reached the next chamber, she stopped short.

There, in the soft glow of ever-burning candles, stood her mother.

Allanagh's silver hair gleamed like moonlight in the dimness. She faced the sarcophagus, her hands resting lightly on its edge, utterly still.

Something in Flur shattered. She ran forward, tears blurring her vision, and flung herself into her mother's arms.

"Flur, what are you doing here?" Allanagh's voice was gentle, threaded with concern, as she held her close, smoothing her hair and murmuring softly until the sobs eased.

Several long moments passed before Flur could speak. "Rhyslin sent me to find you, Mother."

"Why?" Allanagh asked, her brow furrowing as she tipped Flur's chin upward, examining her face.

"The Council of the saor-shealbhadairean will meet in seven days, and they want to review the treaty that you, Aunt Mayana, and Ria made with Rhyslin."

"Mayana is here with me," Allanagh said, one brow lifting. "Ria? Why did Ilyriatri shorten her name?"

Flur hesitated. There was only one reason a woman did that. Before she could answer, she saw the change in her mother's eyes, the softening, the sharp intake of breath.

"Did she bond with him?" Allanagh asked quietly.

Flur nodded.

From the shadows along the far wall, another figure stepped forward. The red-haired queen of the mountain people emerged into the candlelight, wiping discreetly at her eyes. "Did who bond with him? And who is he?"

"Ilyriatri and Mac Draoidheachd," Allanagh replied, though her gaze never left Flur. "When did she do this?"

The weight of the question pressed down on Flur's shoulders. She lowered her head, trying to hide behind her hair.

"Flur."

The single word left no room for evasion.

"About a week after he bonded with me," she whispered.

"Why ever would she do a thing like that?" Mayana asked, stepping closer, disbelief sharp in her voice. "Surely she knew what would happen when she did."

"She knew," Flur said, her stomach tightening beneath their shared scrutiny. "And she didn't care." She swallowed hard. "As to why — it's because she thought he was a ciad-fhir."

Allanagh frowned. "I didn't quite hear that. She thought he was what?"

"Ciad-fhir," Flur repeated, louder now, the word trembling as it left her. "She thought he might be one of the First Men."

Both queens went utterly still.

"Why would she think—?" Allanagh began, glancing toward Mayana.

"Ah," Mayana said softly, her voice gentling. She looked thoughtful rather than surprised. "I suppose if she didn't truly know him, it might make sense."

Flur watched her closely as Mayana continued.

"He's nearly six hundred years old and doesn't look a day over fifty. He has near-perfect control over his prana, and A' Mathair did call him son." Mayana gave a quiet, rueful laugh. "Ilyriatri never wanted to be a queen. She wanted a home, a household, a family. When Garion died, she lost all of that. Maighstir Rhyslin must have seemed like an answer to her prayers."

The words settled heavily in Flur's chest. She had never thought of it that way, not fully. Understanding crept in, slow and painful, and with it a new ache: not jealousy, not anger, but sorrow—for Ria, and for everything she had given up.

Hearing it said aloud, Allanagh nodded slowly. "If she has found what she was looking for, then I'm happy for her." Her sternness melted into a small smile. "Can Sloan come with me?"

Flur blushed, a mischievous glint in her eye. "Yes, Mathair, your maighstir can come with you." She ducked her head as if expecting a playful swat, but none came.

Allanagh only gave her a thoughtful look. "How long have you known? We thought we had hidden it so well."

"For almost ten years, Mathair," Flur admitted softly. "I could tell you loved him. That's why I never fought you over him. He's one of the good ones."

A deep male voice broke the silence, rolling out from the dim recesses of the crypt like a low bell.

"I'm glad to hear that," it said, warm and amused.

Flur turned, startled, as two figures stepped from the shadows. The first was tall and broad-shouldered, his dark hair threaded with silver, his presence filling the air like the scent of rain before a storm.

Sloan's blue eyes caught the candlelight as he smiled. Behind him came another man, slender, slightly older, with a warrior's stillness and a quick, assessing gaze that marked him as one accustomed to danger.

"It would have saved much time if you had just said that earlier," Sloan added, brushing stone dust from his sleeve as if he had been waiting for her to arrive.

"I didn't want to spoil your sneaking about," Flur replied with a grin, the tension easing from her shoulders. "How are you, Sloan?"

"I'm well." He engulfed her in a hug that lifted her from the ground. His armor was cool beneath her cheek, and his laughter rumbled through her bones. "How does being a bhanna suit you?"

"I'm happy," Flur admitted, the glow in her eyes softening her words. She looked past him to the unfamiliar man lingering a few steps back. "Who is this?"

"His name is Silas falt Airgid."

The red-haired Mountain Queen stepped forward, her hand sliding with easy familiarity around the newcomer's arm. Pride and defiance warred in her smile, and Flur felt a faint, startled warmth at the sight, another secret revealed so simply.

"He's my bond," Mayana said, her smirk edged with mischief. "Unlike Allanagh, I kept my bond a secret from even Rhyslin."

Then her expression faltered, the levity slipping away as a new thought took hold. "Where is Ilyriatri?"

"She went to get General Makar," Flur said quietly. The words tasted bitter as she spoke them. "He's going to have to take her place at the council. The Saorsan laws don't allow bonded women to hold power." Her voice darkened despite her effort to keep it steady. "Even if they are a queen."

The torchlight flickered, catching the glance exchanged between Allanagh and Mayana. Flur watched the shift closely, the shared silence, the straightening of shoulders, the familiar hardening of resolve she had seen before battle councils and treaty talks alike.

"Sloan will represent our people in their council," Allanagh said, her voice cutting clean and sharp through the stillness. For a heartbeat, even the air seemed to pause. She looked up at him, her eyes bright as embers. "And he will sign the treaty and lead our people."

Flur's breath caught. The weight of it settled slowly, like a stone placed carefully but deliberately upon her chest.

Sloan's lips curved, a faint spark of challenge glinting in his gaze. "And if I don't?"

The Mountain Queen met his look without flinching, affection and mock irritation blending seamlessly. "If you don't, I'll be the most insufferable bhanna you've ever seen."

She stepped closer. Flur caught the mingled scents of her hair—spice and flowers—threading through the cool, mineral air of the crypt. Mayana's fingers curled around the hilt of his sword, her touch balanced between threat and promise.

"But," she whispered, rising onto her toes to brush a kiss against his lips, "you know that's the best thing for our people."

When Mayana drew back, something softer lay beneath the fire in her eyes. Years of strain showed through the cracks.

"I worry about the Orcan and An fheadhainn a thuit raids," she said quietly. "It's nothing against our army, but we are outnumbered, and I am tired of watching people die."

The words settled heavily in Flur's chest. She had grown up with those fears, heard them whispered in council chambers and cried over in private rooms. Hearing them now, spoken aloud, made them feel suddenly, painfully real.

Sloan exhaled, the sound low and weighted. He drew Mayana close for a moment, his hand resting on her shoulder in silent reassurance.

"You are right, òran mo chridhe," he said gently. Then his gaze shifted past her, toward Silas. "What do you plan to do?"

The other man stepped forward, his boots echoing softly against the stone.

His gray-streaked hair caught the torchlight, and his calm, steady eyes did not waver. "Mayana is stepping down, and I will accept the treaty."

Flur's heart skipped. She hadn't realized she'd been holding her breath until it rushed out of her all at once.

Mayana's eyes narrowed, but Silas met her gaze without hesitation. "If Ilyriatri has stepped down and Makar has taken over, you must do the same thing." His smile was small, tired, but kind. "Bannachian do not lead, and the bonding was your choice."

The truth of it rang through the crypt, stark and unyielding. Flur felt the shape of the future settle into place, not clean, not painless, but necessary. For the first time since she had stepped through the shadows, she believed the treaty might truly hold.

The flame-haired queen lifted her chin. For a heartbeat, pride warred with affection, then she exhaled softly and nodded.

"I know, and I'm sure that Rhyslin will be furious that I kept you a secret from him."

Flur's laughter rang lightly in the crypt, warm against the chill air.

"This amuses you?" Mayana asked, one eyebrow rising in mock severity.

"There was speculation that you'd beg Rhyslin for his bond," Flur giggled. "He'll be relieved to know he won't have to do that now."

Mayana's expression flickered between amusement and offense, prompting Flur to hurry on.

"He would have bonded with you had you asked, but he's sort of got his hands full."

"Oh? Is there a third?" Allanagh asked, curiosity threading through her voice.

Flur nodded brightly. "There is. Her name is Rowena, and she's twenty-four years old and a seeress of Despoina."

The queens exchanged looks, half disbelief, half admiration.

"I refuse to feel sorry for him," Mayana said dryly, though her lips curved with reluctant humor. "For all his protestations of never wanting to bond a woman, he now has three."

"Possibly more," Flur replied, her tone light but mysterious.

At Allanagh's raised eyebrow, she continued, "He has said that if we three can agree on new bonds, he will consider them." The golden-haired bhanna tilted her chin with mock pride. "He's found that having women fuss over him is to his liking."

Silas gave a soft laugh, shaking his head. "That's all good and fine, but how are we going to get to Am Flur Manse in seven days?"

Flur's smile widened as she reached into her pocket and drew out a smooth, opalescent stone that pulsed faintly with inner light. The shadows along the walls seemed to bend toward it.

"With this," she said. "Rhyslin said that once I use this, he'll open a portal to Am Flur Manse." She shivered slightly, the air around her cooling as the stone shimmered. "It'll be a shadow portal and mess with your mind, but if we don't have to concentrate on it, it should be easier than getting here."

"I don't understand," Allanagh said softly, brow furrowing. "Why was it hard to find me?"

"I didn't know where you were. I had to concentrate on you, not a place." Flur's mouth twisted into a small pout. "Do you know how hard that is? All my memories of you are tied up in places where we've lived, spent time, and experienced heartbreaks."

She hugged her mother tightly. "When I finally stopped thinking of places, it was easier to find you, but I didn't expect to find you here," she whispered. "I should have, though. I should have remembered it was time for our pilgrimage to Papa's tomb."

"It's okay," Allanagh murmured, smoothing her daughter's hair. The warmth of her embrace seemed to drive back the chill of the tomb. "If we leave from here, will Rhyslin be able to provide us with clothes and necessities?"

Flur smiled through the tears still clinging to her lashes. "Of course. I'm sure he can provide whatever we need, and if he doesn't have it, he can get it from the nearest town."

"Good," Allanagh said, satisfaction softening her tone. She turned toward Mayana. "Is there any pressing need to return to Caisteal Beinne Uaine?"

When the other woman shook her head, Allanagh looked up at Sloan, her expression open and searching. "What would you have us do, mo chridhe?"

Sloan chuckled low in his throat. "It does a lot of good to ask after you've decided on something," he teased gently. Then his eyes softened, their blue depths bright in the candlelight. "We go to Am Flur Manse, of course."

He turned to Flur, nodding toward the shimmering mind stone in her hand. "Can you let Maighstir Rhyslin know that we are ready?"

The light from the stone flared once, casting long shadows that rippled across the carved walls of Garion's tomb. Light and shadow mingled across the tomb walls, and Flur had the strange sense that something was ending, even as something else waited to begin.

The air in Garion's tomb was heavy with the scent of age and stone dust, still swirling faintly from where the portal had last shimmered. The torches along the walls guttered, their light licking the carved runes that spiraled upward like ivy made of flame. In her hands, the mind stone pulsed with a soft inner glow, as though it drew breath along with her.

Flur lifted it reverently to her heart, her fingers trembling just slightly from exhaustion and awe.

"Yes, Maighstir," she said softly, her voice barely above a whisper. "Maighstir Rhyslin."

The light within the stone deepened to violet-black, and from its depths came his voice, low, rich, and threaded with shadow.

"Yes, mo fhlùr àlainn. Did you find Allanagh?"

Flur's lips parted, but no words came at first. The others watched her, soldiers, queens, and bonds alike, all silent, as though the air itself waited. After a breath, she murmured, "Yes, Maighstir. We're at Papa's tomb, and Mayana is with us."

For a heartbeat, only the torches crackled. Then Rhyslin's voice returned, thoughtful, quieter. "I understand. How many will you be bringing back?"

"Ten, Maighstir," Flur replied, glancing around at the gathered faces. "Momma, Sloan, Mayana, Maighstir Silas falt Airgid, and five soldiers."

A pause, then a trace of curiosity colored his tone. "Silas falt Airgid?" He hesitated, as though searching memory's archives. "Is he about my height, with silver hair and dark eyes?"

When Flur confirmed it, the air around the stone seemed to hum faintly.

"I know him. He was a field commander in Garion's army. Why is he coming?"

Silas stepped closer, his boots scuffing softly against the crypt floor. The old stone seemed to carry his voice when he called out.

"Because I'm bonded to Mayana, General Darkblade."

The silence that followed was tangible, a ripple of surprise that seemed to stretch even through the unseen connection between worlds.

"I see," Rhyslin finally said, his tone neutral but edged with weary amusement. "I look forward to hearing all about it when you arrive."

At once, the air thickened. A low hum gathered in the center of the chamber as shadows began to twist into motion, coiling like smoke drawn into a whirlpool. The floor darkened beneath their feet, stone rippling like inked water.

"I'll hold it open until the last person is through," Rhyslin's voice promised, calm and steady even as the vortex expanded, a spiraling gate of shadow rimmed in faint silver light.

They moved in pairs, as if obeying some ancient ritual. Flur went first, her hand clutching the glowing mind stone, a soldier at her side.

Then came two more soldiers, followed by Allanagh and Sloan, their fingers brushing as they stepped through the veil. Mayana and Silas followed, their silhouettes haloed by the portal's dim shimmer, and at last the final guards entered the void.

Each pair disappeared soundlessly, leaving behind only the echo of footsteps and the whisper of the dying torches.

Flur emerged into moonlight flooding the grand hall of Am Flur Manse.

Rowena waited near the threshold, flanked by four of Rhyslin's servants, their pale dresses stirring in the faint breeze from the still-open vortex. The moment each traveler emerged, the servants guided them aside, speaking softly, their movements precise and reverent.

When the last two soldiers stepped through, the portal sealed itself with a sound like a deep sigh. The sudden quiet felt vast and sacred.

Rhyslin stood a few paces away, arms folded loosely, eyes gleaming with dark amusement. The faint glimmer of the portal's residue still clung to his hair and shoulders like mist. He turned his gaze toward Mayana and lifted one eyebrow.

The flame-haired queen froze, color rising in her cheeks. "Forgive me, mo dhìonadair," she whispered, lowering her eyes. "I was worried that you would leave us to our fate if I told you about Maighstir Silas."

Rhyslin's expression did not change, though something dry edged his patience.

"So, you neglected to tell me about your mate for what—six months, eight?"

"More like a year," Silas said calmly, stepping forward. His voice carried steady confidence. "Would you have still protected us if you had known?"

Rhyslin blinked, surprise flickering briefly across his face before settling into a mild frown. "Of course I would have still protected you," he said firmly. A sigh followed, quieter, more resigned. "I wouldn't have walked on eggshells for that year," he added with a shrug.

Mayana's eyes widened. "So Flur didn't lie? You might have bonded with me if I weren't bonded and had asked?"

Rhyslin turned his gaze toward Flur. It was half stern, half amused—and heat rushed instantly to her cheeks.

"Yes," he said evenly, "I might have, if Flur and Ria agreed." His voice softened. "I promised Garion I would look after the three of you. He would have been amused to see how it all turned out."

Flur swallowed, the weight of that promise settling heavily in her chest.

Rhyslin shifted his attention to Allanagh and Sloan, his expression easing into something almost warm. "Should I call you Rig-Sloan?"

Sloan's face remained composed, though the corner of his mouth twitched.

"I would rather you didn't. I am Allanagh's mate — and have been."

"That was never much of a secret," Rhyslin replied lightly. "I could tell at the Fort."

When Sloan nodded, Rhyslin inclined his head. "It's a pleasure to meet you. You are all welcome in my house and are safe within my walls."

"Thank you, mo dhìonadair," Mayana said softly, stepping closer to Silas.

Flur noticed the way Rhyslin's gaze lingered on the silver-haired soldier, measuring, curious. Silas leaned close to whisper something to Mayana. Whatever he said widened her eyes before her expression softened.

Without hesitation, Mayana sank to her knees before Rhyslin, head bowed.

"Forgive me, please, Maighstir."

Flur's breath caught.

Allanagh frowned, glancing at Sloan. He gave the faintest nod. Then, with composed grace that made Flur's chest tighten, Allanagh stepped forward and knelt beside Mayana.

"Forgive us, please, Maighstir."

Flur stared. Her pulse thundered in her throat as she looked from her mother to her aunt, then up at Rhyslin, who stood quietly, unreadable, and back again.

She had never imagined this. Not this posture. Not this moment.

She silently walked over and stood behind Rhyslin, she couldn't believe what her mother and aunt were doing. Before today, she would have never believed they'd kneel for anyone or any reason.

For a moment, the world seemed to hold its breath. The torches along the walls flickered, their light wavering, and Flur had the strange sensation, no more than a shiver along her spine, that something unseen watched with quiet amusement.

Rhyslin looked down at them, rubbing a hand across his face as he sighed. The sound held more affection than exasperation.

"As if forgiveness was ever in doubt."

A soft laugh rippled through the chamber, warm, distant, unmistakably not human.

Flur felt it more than she heard it, a gentle pressure that eased the tightness in her chest.

Rhyslin's lips curved faintly, as though the sound was familiar to him.

"Come on inside," he said at last, gesturing toward the adjoining chamber where firelight glowed against stone walls. "We still have to rewrite the treaty to account for what's happened." His gaze flicked toward Silas and Sloan. "We can work through the details while the women get settled."

Flur rose with the others, her legs unsteady but her heart lighter. As they followed Rhyslin into the adjoining chamber, the echo of their footsteps softened, swallowed by the crackle of the hearth.

Warmth spread slowly through her hands and feet, chasing away the chill of the tomb. For the first time since stepping into the shadows, she felt the weight of the journey settle, not as burden, but as proof she had survived it.

Somewhere behind them, the last trace of divine laughter faded.

Flur drew a steady breath and crossed the threshold, unsure of what waited next, but no longer afraid to find out.

Chapter Two

The Coming of the Forest Queen

The morning broke pale and cold, mist curling through the courtyards of Am Flur Manse like low-breathing ghosts. Dew silvered the grass, and the stones of the old terrace still held the night's chill. From the eastern tower, faint light spilled down upon the circle of the portal stone—a great slab of veined marble etched with sigils that glimmered faintly in the dawn.

Rhyslin moved quickly but unhurriedly through the halls, fastening the clasp of his cloak with one hand and holding a steaming egg sandwich in the other. The scent of toasted bread and herbs followed him like an afterthought of mortal comfort.

He looked more scholar than savior that morning, hair unbound, sleeves rolled, but the staff he carried whispered otherwise.

The blackwood stave tapped softly on the flagstones as he approached the portal stone.

By the time he reached it, the sigils carved into its surface were already pulsing with light, a slow rhythm like the beat of a great heart beneath the earth. The air around the stone shimmered faintly, distorting the mist. Then, with a sound like a sigh and the rush of air drawn through silk, a silver gateway sprang into existence.

Rhyslin leaned on his staff, chewing absently as the light gathered and swirled. A faint hum filled the air, resonating in the bones, neither hostile nor benign. He studied the forming gate, narrowing his eyes as recognition teased at him. Familiar, he thought, but why?

A flicker of worry crossed his mind. Ria didn't return last night. The realization settled uneasily in his chest.

He watched the swirling silver deepen to white, then to the shimmer of quicksilver. The smell of ozone and wet earth filled the air, the scent of power gathering.

He took another bite, finished the sandwich, and wiped his hand on the edge of his cloak just as footsteps crunched softly on the gravel behind him.

He glanced over his shoulder to find Rana standing at the edge of the courtyard, early light catching in her dark braid. Her hand rested on the hilt of her sword, eyes fixed on the portal.

"Aren't you supposed to be on your way to Marcus' shack?" Rhyslin asked, voice calm but curious.

"Yes, Maighstir," Rana replied, her tone clipped as she continued to stare at the gateway. Silver light played across her face, painting her features in ghostly hues. "I was about to leave when I heard about this gate." She quirked an eyebrow, wry humor flickering beneath her tension. "Were you expecting something like this?"

"No," Rhyslin admitted, setting his staff upright and resting both hands on it. "I was expecting to hear from your mother today, but nothing like this."

Rana's fingers curled tighter around her sword hilt, knuckles pale. The hum from the gate grew stronger, a vibration that trembled through the flagstones. "Who does it belong to?"

"I don't know," Rhyslin said quietly, eyes never leaving the rippling silver. He could feel it now—not danger exactly, but intent. Something was on the other side, testing the threshold. He flicked a glance toward

Rana. "You might wish you had already left. If this turns into a fight—"

He paused, the futility of sending her away unspoken but heavy.

"If something happens, return to the house and make sure our guests are safe. Make sure the guards don't do anything stupid."

Rana snorted softly. "As if they'd listen to me. They'd do what almost every other man has done — say one thing, then do what they thought was right."

Rhyslin smiled faintly. She wasn't wrong. His men were trained to think independently, a blessing and a curse both. "If I tell you to run, run."

"Yes, Maighstir," she agreed. Her tone was obedient, but her jaw tightened.

The gateway's shimmer intensified, mist whipping outward in rippling spirals. Rhyslin's eyes narrowed. As it solidified, the portal took on a more defined shape: a silver picketed gate, delicate as spun moonlight, bound by a golden-green lock that pulsed faintly like the heart of a leaf.

The sight stirred something deep in his memory. He'd seen that leaf-heart seal before.

Behind him, Rana shifted her stance, then shifted again, too often, as if searching for footing that didn't feel exposed. His admission had unsettled her. The weight of the unknown pressed down like a storm waiting to break.

Then, with a final resonant pulse, the gateway opened.

A cool wind spilled through, fragrant with rain and the sweet scent of forest leaves. Two figures stepped through, dryads, tall and graceful, their long gowns fluttering as though stirred by unseen breezes. Light rippled over their skin in faint patterns of bark and vine, and their eyes glowed softly green in the morning gloom.

When they saw Rhyslin, they lowered themselves immediately, kneeling with heads bowed. One spoke, her voice soft as rustling leaves. "Mac Draoidheachd, may we step fully onto your grounds?"

Her eyes, bright as spring moss, lifted to meet his. Rhyslin blinked, recognition dawning. "Ciara?" he said, startled. When she nodded, he turned to the other. "Marissa, right?"

The second dryad smiled, and that was all the proof he needed. Memories clicked into place—their laughter in Astinmah's groves, their songs among flowering oaks. Of course.

The light within the portal flared again. This time, two tall men stepped through, and the shift in the air was immediate, heavier, sharper, like the moment before lightning strikes.

They stood over six feet tall, salt-and-pepper hair cropped close, scars tracing lines of battle across their faces. Steel armor gleamed like stormlight; blades hung at their sides. Their eyes swept the courtyard with soldierly precision as they moved, each step deliberate, silent, measured.

Without a word, they took position on either side of the portal, scanning for danger. A low hum rolled outward from them—a spiritual pressure so dense it rippled the air.

Rhyslin inhaled, letting the pressure wash over him. It pressed like a deep-sea current, testing his strength but not overwhelming him.

Behind him, Rana gasped and dropped to one knee, her sword clattering softly against the stones. Sweat broke across her brow as she struggled to stay upright. "Who are they?" she managed, voice trembling.

"They are Ciad-fhir," Rhyslin said quietly, eyes narrowing in thought. Astinmah's elite. That alone told him there was a threat.

Rana gritted her teeth and tried to rise, but her muscles trembled under the weight of their presence. "This is what Mother thought you were?" she gasped, disbelief coloring her voice. The prana radiating from them crushed her lungs, driving her breath shallow.

Rhyslin's gaze met that of one guardian, cold, assessing, sharp as tempered steel. Recognition flickered there.

"Fancy meeting you here, Elmir."

The taller guardian's expression didn't shift. "Mac Draoidheachd." His tone was cool, formal, an acknowledgment, not a greeting.

The second guardian's eyes swept the tree line, posture alert, as though expecting attack.

Rhyslin tilted his head, curiosity threading his tone. "Since when does Mathair need two protectors?"

"Since a prisoner escaped from Chloigeann," Elmir rumbled, voice like distant thunder. "We decided to keep Lady Astinmah safe when she travels."

Rhyslin nodded, his earlier conversation with Ananke and Despoina resurfacing. The spider god was free; that much was certain. What none of them knew was whether he had escaped—or been released. His voice sharpened. "Mathair is coming here? Why?"

Elmir didn't flinch. "One of your bhanna requested a portal back to you from her manor house. A' Mathair granted it willingly and wished to meet with you." He glanced around once more, then raised his voice. "Mathair Astinmah, it is safe."

The air brightened. Silver light deepened into gold and green, and the scent of living things, sap, flowers, and deep loam rolled outward. The dryads bowed low.

The Ciad-fhir straightened. Even the birds in the hedgerow fell silent.

Then Mathair Astinmah stepped through.

She came in quiet splendor, light cascading around her like sunlight through leaves. Greenish-gray hair was gathered high in a loose bun, crowned with woven garlands shimmering faintly with dew. Her emerald gown, silver-threaded, clung like living silk, slipping from her shoulders and trailing into the grass, where its train seemed to take root among moss and wildflowers.

Every motion carried the grace of growing things, patient, inevitable, alive. The scent of rain and roses filled the courtyard as her bare feet touched the grass.

Rhyslin straightened, the faintest smile curving his lips as their gazes met.

She paused, luminous green eyes ancient and kind, then smiled with a joy that made the centuries between them feel suddenly small. Astinmah the Nurturer walked forward, arms open.

When she reached him, she embraced him warmly. "Mac mo ghràidh."

Rhyslin returned the embrace, holding her close with quiet affection. "Mathair. What brings you here?"

The air shimmered faintly as the portal's silver light faded into the gray calm of morning. Mist lingered low, curling around the dryads' feet. The scent of loam and crushed blossoms clung to the space she had crossed.

"Surely Elmir told you," Astinmah replied, warmth threaded with gentle reproach. She cast the Ciad-fhir a sidelong glance, faint green light gleaming in her eyes.

"He did," Rhyslin said, "but I wanted to hear it from you."

Her brow furrowed. "Don't you trust—?" The question lingered, softer than intended.

"I trust him as much as he trusts me," Rhyslin replied evenly.

Elmir inclined his head in silent agreement. The precise, soldierly gesture seemed to settle the air. Astinmah blinked, then shook off her confusion, garlands swaying faintly like leaves in a breeze.

"Your Ria and her General requested enough power to open a portal. I granted it." Her tone softened, then wavered. "And I wished to speak with you."

Before the words fully settled, the gateway rippled again.

The silver thinned to pale gold, and Ria stepped through, desert-touched beauty radiant against the dimness, followed closely by General Makar, whose armor caught the dawn like a dull mirror.

Rhyslin's desert rose smiled as she approached, brushing a stray lock from her face before pressing a brief kiss onto his cheek. The scent of sand and cedar clung to her, the smell of home carried across impossible distance.

Behind her, Makar's eyes never stopped moving. He surveyed the courtyard, the Ciad-fhir, and Rhyslin himself, jaw set with the vigilance of a man who'd seen too many betrayals to rest easily. The look he sent Rhyslin promised words later, the kind reserved for closed doors.

Rhyslin inclined his head, a ghost of a smile playing on his lips. After a moment, he gestured toward the inner hall.

Makar followed Ria inside, his posture stiff with duty rather than deference.

As the pressure of divine presence eased, the Ciad-fhir drawing back, the dryads relaxing, Rana slipped away. She darted to her mother, wrapped her in a fleeting hug, then ran down the path toward Marcus' shack, laughter trailing behind her like birdsong after storm.

Now only Rhyslin, the Ciad-fhir, and the dryads remained. Morning stillness returned, fragile, as though holding its breath.

Astinmah stepped closer, gown whispering like wind through reeds. She brushed her fingers along Rhyslin's cheek, the touch warm, motherly, faintly trembling.

"Did you hear what happened?"

He shook his head, small and deliberate. He wanted to hear it from her.

"Something interfered with the bonds between Diathan, Taghta, and our followers for nearly a quarter rotation."

A hush fell. Even the birds paused.

Rhyslin drew her gently into his arms. Wildflowers, spring rain, and faint incense wrapped around him. For a moment, she felt less goddess than weary woman seeking solace.

"It was most distressing," she murmured against his cloak. "Almost as if everyone vanished."

"Whatever it was, it didn't affect me," Rhyslin said calmly, eyes darkening with thought. "Did you learn what caused it?"

She stepped back, gathering herself. "No. Quetzalcoatl suspects a new diathan. Ananke and Despoina visited Chloigeann. A trickster was released."

A breeze stirred, cold with stone and iron.

"What I don't understand," she continued, "is why he hasn't revealed himself."

"Do we know who it was?" Rhyslin asked.

"Not definitively. Ananke believes it was a dia fireann named Iktomi."

At the name, Rhyslin's gaze drifted to the fog-softened tree line. "If I had escaped Chloigeann," he said slowly, "I'd stay hidden and gather followers. I'd avoid a fight, like you do."

Astinmah smiled faintly. "I never fight. That's why they are here."

"All the more reason," Rhyslin said. "Iktomi won't want your guardians finding him too soon."

She considered, then sighed. "You may be right. Thank you for listening."

Light returned to the courtyard, mist thinning as though the world exhaled. She smiled freely now—fondness, pride, relief shining through.

She adjusted her garland, the small vanity endearing. Then she hugged him once more.

"Take care, my son. We are pleased with you. All of us, save Despoina, who still can't find your destiny."

Rhyslin raised one eyebrow, amused. She laughed softly.

"Be well, Mother," he said. "Please keep me informed."

"I will."

The portal flared green-gold once more. Dryads followed. The Ciad-fhir lingered, then vanished.

Silence fell.

Only flowers' scent remained. Rhyslin stood alone, sigils of his stave glowing faintly, the weight of what was coming settling over him like the last of the dawn mist.

Chapter Three

Of the Willow and the Blade

Rana took the chance to escape the Ciad-Fhir, following her mother long enough to hug her before taking off toward Marcus' shack. The air was still sharp from the dawn, and her breath misted before her as she sprinted along the gravel path that curved around the mansion's eastern wing. The great house loomed behind her like a silent sentinel, its pale walls gilded faintly by the rising sun.

When she reached the far side, she stopped and bent double, planting her hands on her knees. Her heart thudded in her chest, and the cool air burned her lungs as she tried to steady her breath.

The echo of divine power still lingered in her bones, a residual tremor from standing too near the Ciad-Fhir. *How strong they were,* she thought, a flicker of awe mingling with unease. *Could Maighstir Rhyslin even best them?*

A faint breeze stirred the fallen leaves, carrying the earthy scent of wet loam and pine needles. When her pulse slowed, she knelt and brushed aside a patch of dead grass and brittle leaves until bare soil showed through, a circle of ground devoid of life, perfect for sigil work.

Dropping to one knee, she drew the point of her finger through the dirt, tracing each curling rune with the care of a scribe. The symbols glimmered faintly in the morning light, as though they recognized her touch.

Closing her eyes, she recalled Rhyslin's lessons: *imagine the map, the room, the destination, until it feels like you are already there.*

Rana pictured Marcus' domain as best she could, the mark he'd carved into the parchment map in Rhyslin's study, the faint scent of cedar ink that had lingered over it. She steadied her breathing, letting her imagination pull her toward the spot she'd never seen. Then, pricking her fingertip with a small knife, she let a single drop of blood fall onto the sigil.

For a long moment, nothing happened. The forest around her seemed to hold its breath. Then the lines in the soil began to shimmer with silver light, spreading outward like ripples across still water.

The air grew taut with energy, the scent of ozone mingling with damp earth, and the space above the sigil folded inward, condensing into a sphere of swirling silver.

The sphere expanded, and within it appeared a vision of another place, a lone black willow standing on a grassy hilltop beneath a slate-colored sky. Its branches hung long and low, whispering secrets to the wind.

Rana drew in a breath, heart hammering. Then, gathering her courage, she sprinted forward and leapt into the light.

The world folded.

For an instant, she felt weightless, neither falling nor flying, before her boots struck solid ground once more. The portal's glow faded behind her, vanishing with a faint sigh, leaving her alone beneath the great willow.

The tree's long boughs swayed gently in the breeze, their tips brushing her shoulders like ghostly fingers. A chorus of unseen insects hummed in the tall grass, and the air was thick with the scent of sap and moss.

Rana turned in a slow circle, taking in her surroundings. A little distance away, half-hidden in a copse of birches, stood a small hunting shack. Its roof was patched with moss, smoke curling faintly from a narrow stone chimney. A line of drying herbs hung under the eaves, swaying like pendants in the morning air.

"This must be the place," Rana whispered to herself. "If I'm in the wrong place, Maighstir Rhyslin can open a gate for me."

Her hazel eyes swept the hilltop, alert for any movement. Not seeing anyone, she began to step away from the tree. "Surely I'm in the right place."

"You're in the right place," a voice called down from above.

Rana's hand flew to the hilt of her sword as she spun toward the sound. Her gaze climbed the willow's dark branches until she spotted movement, a figure perched high above, half-veiled by swaying fronds. The speaker dropped lightly from her perch, landing in a low crouch that sent up a puff of dust.

The girl before her appeared to be a young *teine*, lithe and quick, poised between childhood and womanhood.

Her green eyes sparkled like sunlit emeralds beneath a mane of fiery red hair that tumbled over her shoulders. The faint scent of wildflowers and smoke clung to her.

"You're noisy," the girl said, rising to her full height and fixing Rana with a piercing look.

"I'm sorry. I didn't mean to be noisy," Rana replied quickly, then hesitated, realizing she didn't know why she felt compelled to apologize. Her gaze dropped to the girl's clothing, a dark green blouse, a brown skirt that fell to mid-thigh, and black leggings tucked into well-worn leather boots. Every stitch spoke of movement, not vanity.

"You can't help it," the girl said as she began circling Rana like a cat assessing a newcomer. The faint crunch of dry grass followed her steps. "You were almost late, and Father will want to know why."

"Father?" Rana echoed, still catching her breath. "I was supposed to meet Maighstir Marcus. I am in the right place, yes?"

"You are. I'm Angelica. Marcus is my father." The girl's tone softened, curiosity lighting her features. "What's your name?"

"Um— Rana. My name is Rana," she answered, silently cursing herself for stammering. "Maighstir Rhyslin said you were about to undergo your trials." She blinked. "How old are you?"

Angelica's grin was bright and mischievous. "I'm sixteen." Her eyes flicked down to Rana's attire, and she nodded approvingly. "At least you dressed right." Then, with sudden movement, she darted down the hill, her laughter ringing through the trees. "Come on, follow me."

Rana broke into an easy lope behind her, adjusting her pace to match the girl's. Angelica moved like quicksilver, slipping between trees, vaulting fallen logs, barely disturbing the grass beneath her feet. Rana found herself smiling despite the exertion.

The forest around them was alive with the hum of morning: birdcalls echoing through the canopy, the chatter of squirrels, the distant murmur of a stream.

By the time they reached the shack, Rana's breathing had steadied again. Angelica, still full of restless energy, bounded up the small steps and rapped her knuckles against the door. "Daddy, I found her! She was at the top of the hill under the black willow," she announced eagerly, her voice bright as bells. "And she was noisy."

From within came a rich, even voice, calm but edged with authority. "Very well, Sweetling. Go find me a silver-haired sionnaich, follow it to its den, and then draw me a map to the location, complete with distance, height, and water notations."

The redhead's face lit with excitement. "Yes, Father. I'll be back when I've found it." She rolled her eyes and laughed as Marcus ruffled her hair through the doorway. "If you get a chance, you can join me, Rana."

Angelica threw her arms around Rana in a quick, exuberant hug that smelled faintly of sun-warmed pine needles. "See ya later," she said, before dashing off into the forest beyond the shack, her footsteps soon swallowed by the sound of rustling leaves.

Marcus watched his daughter disappear into the forest, her laughter fading into the rustle of branches and birdsong. For a moment, the quiet returned, broken only by the distant sigh of the wind through the tall pines and the faint creak of the shack's weathered boards behind him. A gray light filtered through the canopy, mottling the ground with shifting patches of shadow.

He turned to Rana, his expression calm but assessing, eyes sharp as a hawk's beneath the brim of his hood. The faint scent of pine resin and damp earth hung between them.

"You were almost late."

Rana straightened, her cheeks flushed from the run and the residual heat of her portal crossing. "I know, Maighstir Marcus, but Maighstir Rhyslin had an unexpected guest." Her voice was quiet, almost deferential.

She opened her mouth to say more, but Marcus lifted a hand, the gesture as economical as the man himself. "Unexpected guest?"

Rana nodded. "A silver gate appeared in his backyard, and when it opened, a pair of dryads danced out and knelt at his feet. Then, two ciad-fhir showed up to guard the gate."

Marcus's brow furrowed. A faint breeze stirred his dark hair, tugging at the edges of his cloak. "Why would two ciad-fhir be guarding a gate?"

"Because they were guarding A' Mathair. Lady Astinmah brought Momma back from Comraich uisge na gealaich." She took a steadying breath before continuing, her tone hushed with remembered awe. "The ciad-fhir are powerful. I had no choice but to kneel and couldn't get to my feet."

Marcus's eyes narrowed thoughtfully. "Did A' Mathair say why she was being escorted?"

Rana shrugged, the motion small but weary. "When momma took Makar inside, I took my chance and got away from the ciad-fhir, then came straight here."

For a long heartbeat, Marcus said nothing. A sparrow chattered somewhere nearby; a leaf fell, spiraling down between them. Then he exhaled through his nose, slow and measured, and tapped a calloused finger against his thigh, the soft rhythm of thought.

Something in her posture reminded him how new she still was. "It's okay," he said finally, voice gentling. "I'll ask Rhyslin about it later."

A rare smile touched his face, the hard lines easing. "Are you ready to get to work?"

Relief washed across her face like sunlight breaking through cloud. "Yes, Maighstir Marcus, I'm ready."

"Good." He crossed his arms over his chest, cloak shifting with the motion. "We'll start by seeing what your swordsmanship is like. Then we'll move to archery and wilderness survival and tracking."

Rana nodded immediately, coming to attention. The soft leather of her boots whispered against the packed soil as she shifted her stance. Her back leg fell just behind her front, her feet shoulder-width apart. One hand rested lightly on the hilt of her sword, the other relaxed at her side. Her hazel eyes, bright with both respect and determination, never left Marcus's face.

"Maighstir Rhyslin is having me train with Rembran," she offered.

"How did your first lesson go?"

She winced slightly. "I lost, but barely." A faint smile ghosted across her lips. "Like Rhyslin, he cheated, but I expected that."

Marcus nodded, a knowing gleam in his eye. "Life on the battlefield is rarely fair."

Rana rolled her eyes in quiet amusement, and he chuckled, the sound low and warm.

"Heard that one already, have you?" When she nodded, he tilted his head. "Who do you think taught it to Rhyslin?"

Rana blinked, a flicker of curiosity crossing her face. She kept silent a moment, studying him, this man older than Rhyslin, older perhaps than she could guess.

The air between them smelled faintly of woodsmoke and steel. "I didn't know, Maighstir," she admitted softly, then after a pause: "Have you always 'cheated' to win?"

Marcus's laughter came easy and unforced, echoing faintly in the still air. "Life is only fair if you've settled on the rules ahead of time." His eyes caught the morning light, glinting amber. "Otherwise, you fight with what you bring to the battlefield. Some fight with every weapon on the field, some use bows, some use swords, and some only use magic. Some, like Rembran, use swords, shields, and magic. Some, like Rhyslin, use the very world against you."

He paused, the wind sighing softly through the trees, and added more quietly, "And don't get me started on nan Diathan. They bring entire worlds and stars with them."

"How do people survive battle like that?" Rana asked, her tone a blend of awe and dismay.

"By hiding until it's over," Marcus said simply. The matter-of-factness in his voice left no room for illusion.

She hesitated, then: "So, what should I bring to the battlefield?" Despite her uncertainty, curiosity pushed her onward.

"Whatever you think you can use to stay alive," he answered, his gaze steady but kind.

Rana drew in a quiet breath, her resolve hardening.

She returned to her stance, every muscle poised. "What would you like me to do, Maighstir?"

Marcus shifted, leaning back against the shack's rough timber wall. The faint creak of wood and the smell of old smoke accompanied the motion. "Run through your sword drill. I'll watch and correct any flaws."

Rana inclined her head in acknowledgment and stepped into the open patch of ground before the cabin. The soil was soft beneath her boots, dust rising faintly as she moved. She wrapped her fingers around her sword's hilt; the leather grip felt cool and familiar in her palm.

Without conscious thought, she drew her blade, the sound of steel whispering from its sheath. The motion began slow, almost reverent: *whispering breeze*, a rising arc that cut through the sunlight filtering between branches.

Her body flowed into *rising dust devil*, halting at shoulder level, a stance of poised potential.

A half step forward, and the movement shifted, the upward sweep collapsing into *iron glove*, her blade vertical before her face. She held it, breath steady, then brought it down in a sharp, fluid stroke: *lightning strike.* The blade hissed through the air, leaving a faint shimmer of disturbed dust in its wake.

At the end of the slash, she pivoted smoothly, turning the edge downward—*catch-claw.* The sword's point dipped toward the earth before snapping upward into *snake bite*, the steel flashing pale in the morning light.

She stepped back, light on her feet, retreating from an imagined foe.

The sequence carried her forward without pause, breath flowing with motion. When she settled into *snake skin*, coiled and ready, her knee bent and the blade draped down her back, Marcus gave a single, precise nod.

Rana exhaled and slid the sword into its sheath. The metallic click sounded final.

"Very good," Marcus said. "Eriand Silver-blade taught you well."

Her mouth quirked, pride held in check.

"Now," he added, drawing his own sword with a single effortless motion, "let's see what you can do against me."

The forest seemed to quiet.

Wind shifted through the trees, carrying damp moss and pine resin. The clearing fell into a hush that pressed against her ears.

They faced each other.

Then they moved.

Raven's wing met short guard—steel kissed steel with a sharp hiss, sparks flickering between them. Rana angled her blade from her waist, pivoted, let his edge slide free, and dipped low to her right as leaves scattered beneath her boots.

Parting the reeds swept up from her hip, fast and precise.

Marcus countered with *falling rain*, his blade sliding down to deflect hers. The impact sent a tremor up her arm, but she recovered instantly. His sword hooked hers wide, then reversed in *thresh the field*, driving toward her open center.

Rana dove aside. Dirt and pine needles bit her palms as she rolled and came up in *descending window*, hilt raised at eye level, blade angled down like a shard of glass.

"You almost got me," she said, breath quick but steady.

Descending window collapsed into *lightning strike*. Her blade split the air with a whistle sharp enough to make Marcus step back, his brows drawing together.

"Nice move," he said. "That's new."

She didn't answer.

Lightning strike flowed into *splitting the sheave*. Her momentum carried her forward, the sword's tip snagging the edge of his cloak and tearing free a thread of fabric.

The air rippled.

Marcus vanished.

Rana froze.

The forest rustled—empty, wrong. Her heart thudded once, hard.

Accidental magic, she thought grimly.

She could still feel him—not seen, but present, like the pressure before a storm.

Fine. Two can play that game.

She traced a sigil in the loam with her toe and whispered,

"Bris an solas gu dathan, nochd am fear falaichte[1]."

Light flared along her blade, refracting into rippling hues—crimson, violet, emerald—spinning as she turned slowly in place.

Something flickered to her left.

A shimmer bent where no air should bend.

There.

She dropped low, boots silent on the soft earth, moving on cat's paws. Each step was measured, breath shallow. She slid behind him and lifted her sword.

Splitting the sheave.

Marcus's blade snapped up just in time. Steel rang, bright and sharp, the force jolting her wrists.

She adjusted instantly.

Her left foot flicked.

------

[1] Break the light into many colors and uncover what is hidden

A small stone leapt from the dirt and spun toward his face.

"Briseadh agus fras![2]"

The stone shattered midair with a thundercrack, exploding into glittering shards.

Marcus swore and rolled back. The fragments rang against his bracers and tore faint lines through leather. He hit a tree hard, bark scraping beneath his shoulders, then vaulted upward, catching a low branch.

Rana looked up just as he ran along it.

She struck.

Lightning detonated where he had been a heartbeat before. White light blinded the clearing, thunder ripping through the forest as charred wood rained down.

He was already moving.

Rana pivoted, tracking him through the trees—too fast, too high. Her lungs burned as she turned, searching for the next opening.

[3]Something tugged her ankle.

She looked down.

------

[2] Break and Shatter!

Vine.

It coiled once, then twice—slick and relentless—winding around her leg, then her thigh.

Another loop snared her arm, yanking her sword tight against her chest. She gasped as it climbed higher, constricting her ribs, her shoulders, her throat.

She struggled, breath turning shallow as the vine dragged her to her knees. Bark scraped her skin through her leggings.

Not fair, she thought wildly.

"I yield!" she coughed.

The pressure eased.

Marcus dropped lightly from the tree. His shadow fell across her.

"If it's any consolation," he said, brushing wood dust from his cloak, "you nearly had me. One more weather strike and I would've been on the ground."

The vine tightened again, squeezing her ribs.

Marcus frowned. "That'll do." He tapped it once. "Let her go."

The vine resisted—a low, humming vibration passed through the earth—then loosened and slid away, pooling at his feet.

Rana sucked in air and rubbed her arms where red marks bloomed.

"Is it alive?" she asked hoarsely.

"In a way," Marcus said. "It remembers what it was made to do."

She stared at the vine, exhaustion warring with wonder. "That's... amazing."

He glanced at her. "You're not going to complain about fairness?"

She shook her head slowly. "No." Her voice steadied. "I've realized I'll never beat a man head-on. I want to learn how to survive. Escape. Run away." She lifted her eyes to his. "The only way I'll win is by being sneaky."

The forest stirred, leaves whispering overhead.

Marcus watched her sheath her sword, the motion deliberate, resolved. Then he nodded once.

"I can teach you that," he said. "It's what I've been teaching Angelica."

A tired, genuine smile touched Rana's lips.

The clearing settled back into quiet, the crackle of magic fading into the living pulse of the woods.

Chapter Four

Of Old Friends and New Bonds

The goddess and her attendants vanished as swiftly as a gust of wind, leaving only the echo of their presence behind. The air in the yard still shimmered faintly, the grass bending as if bowing to where divinity had stood. A thin veil of warmth clung to the place, fading slowly into the cool breath of the afternoon.

Rhyslin remained where he was, the stave resting against his shoulder. For a long moment, he said nothing. The yard felt too large now, too quiet, the sighing of leaves and the faint hum of wards the only sounds left behind. His gaze dropped to the stave, to the runes carved deep into its surface.

He traced one with his finger, absently, almost reverently, feeling the faint pulse of lingering magic beneath his skin—like the echo of a heartbeat already gone.

Astinmah's warning stirred again in his thoughts, the name she had spoken like distant thunder. A new god. A chaos god, perhaps. His lips pressed thin. The last time chaos had walked Crann na Beatha, the world itself had shifted. If the goddess spoke true, the peace they had woven could unravel faster than he could mend it.

A deliberate cough broke the quiet behind him.

Rhyslin blinked and turned. Makar stood at the edge of the yard, framed by the stone archway, posture rigid, face dark as a gathering storm. His cloak stirred in the breeze, iron fittings catching the pale sunlight.

"I would have words with you, old friend."

Still half adrift in the wake of divinity, Rhyslin blinked again, slow this time, missing at first the flicker beneath Makar's scowl. "About?"

"About you kidnapping our Banrig and forcing a bond on her."

The words landed like gravel. Rhyslin took in the exaggerated stance—the puffed chest, the clenched fists— and something didn't quite fit. Still, the accusation struck deeper than the performance suggested.

"Makar," Rhyslin said softly, disbelief cutting through his voice before he could stop it. "Do you believe that I would ever do anything like that?"

The silence that followed stretched, heavy and sharp. Rhyslin watched Makar closely, noting the tension at the corners of his mouth, the way his gaze lingered just a fraction too long.

"It doesn't matter what I think, old friend," Makar said at last, his tone solemn to the point of parody. "The fact is that I sent a Banrigh to Trì aibhnichean daingneach, and not only did she not return, but when she did, she was bonded to a man that I thought was my friend."

He shook his head, sorrow laid on thick. "Rig-Garion would be disappointed in you, old friend."

Rhyslin bowed his head. Shadows pooled across his features as clouds drifted overhead. "If you believe that I have done this thing," he said quietly, "then you might as well put that sword through my heart."

He lifted his gaze again, eyes steady, unreadable. "For if I have forced yon woman against her will, then you are honor bound to end my existence."

A beat passed.

Then Rhyslin saw it—the telltale spark behind Makar's eyes, the barely restrained mirth that betrayed him.

"Leis na diathan uile," Makar muttered, shaking his head. "When did you figure it out?"

Rhyslin's lips twitched. "That you were pulling my leg?"

When Makar nodded, Rhyslin allowed himself a small, knowing smile.
"When you didn't unsheathe your blade."

He stepped closer and laid a hand on Makar's shoulder, the familiar weight of armor warm beneath his palm, the contact heavy with shared history.

"What did Ria tell you, in truth?"

Makar grunted, the tension easing from his stance. "Yon woman told me that she knelt at your feet and begged you to bond with her. She said it was a close contest about who would be first, Flur or her."

Rhyslin chuckled, the sound low and tired, as though wrung from long days and longer nights.

"She graciously let Flur go first, then bonded with me a week later."

He released Makar's shoulder, his gaze softening as the moment settled.

"I had no idea what I was getting myself into," he added quietly, "and I haven't been the same since."

The wind shifted, carrying the scent of distant rain. Makar's shoulders eased. The scowl melted from his face, and to Rhyslin it looked like something gentler surfaced there, the familiar shadow of old grief eased by long friendship. "Ria loves you, old friend. I haven't seen her happy since Garion died, and from what I could tell, Rana is also happier."

Rhyslin snorted. "I must have been blind, my friend, because I didn't know that Allanagh and Mayana were also bonded. Had I known that the treaties would have been written differently, I would have just needed three signatures: yours, Sloan's, and Silas'. The treaties would have been filed as soon as I turned them in. But because I thought we were dealing with three Hin I-Balanath Banrighrean, the full council would have wanted to speak to them before accepting the treaties."

"How could you know that Allanagh was bhanna? You haven't seen her since Garion's death." Makar's voice softened. "I think you have a right to be upset with Mayana. You became her protector, and she still hid the bonding from you."

Rhyslin gave a dry laugh, shaking his head. "I'm just glad we hadn't shared a bed. That just wouldn't be right."

"Ye're right," Makar agreed, lips twitching. "So, what are our plans for the council meeting?"

Rhyslin took a slow, deliberate breath. The yard smelled of turned earth and cedar oil from the stave. "I introduce Silas, Sloan, and you to the council, advise them that you want to join the Saorsa, and stand back as they talk to you three. I plan to watch as you three sign the treaties and your people become part of the Saorsa."

Makar nodded, the wind tugging at his cloak. "That sounds good to me. Why don't we break this to the rest?"

"Are you sure you don't want to run me through first?" Rhyslin said with mock solemnity.

"Ifrinn, no." The general's grin flashed beneath his beard. "Ria would never forgive me, and I'd have to constantly watch my back to make sure Rana didn't kill me." His eyes glinted. "I could nick you and take my 'bloody' sword into Ria."

Rhyslin's expression flattened. "Are you trying to get me killed? Ria would never forgive me, and I'd have to watch my back. It wouldn't just be Rana after me. Flur and Rowena would make my life miserable." He shuddered in exaggerated dread.

Makar laughed, the sound booming and bright against the quiet yard. A pair of sparrows took flight from the eaves.

"I find it odd that you've bonded three women," he said offhandedly.

"As if I had a choice," Rhyslin grumbled, though the faintest smile tugged at the corner of his mouth. "Once I bonded with Flur, I had no choice but to bond with Rowena. Ria was a pleasant surprise. She's the calm center of my little family."

Makar snorted, nostalgia softening his tone. "Not surprising. She was the same for Garion's little family.

All the lass wanted to do was stay home and tend to her new family."

"So I've heard," Rhyslin said with a grin. He turned toward the mansion, the late sun casting long shadows across the yard. "Let's head back inside and see what we need to do."

As Makar stepped beside him, their boots crunched softly over gravel.

Behind them, the wind stirred the runes on the stave, faintly glowing as if in approval—old magic listening, and remembering.

◆ ◆ ◆

Rhyslin and Makar had no sooner stepped inside than warmth and light washed over them. The air of the foyer was rich with the scent of polished wood, burning cedar, and the faint trace of herbs drifting from some distant hearth. Afternoon sunlight streamed through high windows, painting golden bars across the marble floor and the two men who crossed it. The hush of the great house was broken at once by the flutter of skirts and quick, familiar voices.

Rhyslin's three bhanna descended like a storm of color and concern.

"Are you okay, Mo Maighstir?" Flur inquired as she circled him, eyes sharp and worried, her fingers brushing over the folds of his robe to check for wounds. The motion stirred the faint perfume of heather that always clung to her hair.

"If he had been injured, M'Lady Despoina would have told me," Rowena interjected from the other side, her dark hair catching the light like a raven's wing. Her tone was edged with certainty, though her eyes searched him all the same.

Ria rolled her eyes, the motion gentle, affectionate. "How could she do that, considering that she can't see his destiny?"

The seeress paused mid-breath, then dug back, "I would have known." She softened, the certainty in her voice fading to tenderness as she wrapped her arms around Rhyslin's waist.

His shoulders eased beneath her touch, and for a

moment the clamor stilled, replaced by the low rustle of fabric and the faint creak of old wood.

Satisfied that Rhyslin was unharmed, Flur turned toward Makar. Her long golden hair slipped over her shoulder like a spill of sunlight. "Are you injured, Maighstir Makar?" Her blue eyes sparkled as she stepped forward and knelt at his feet, the hem of her gown brushing the polished stone.

"Umm. No, I'm not injured, ciad-bhann Flur." His voice came out rougher than he intended, and Rhyslin noted the faint hesitation in him as the old soldier shifted beneath her attention. He smiled awkwardly, the sound of his armor faintly creaking as he turned to Ria while the others drifted from the room.

"Darna Bann Ria, I wish you happiness," Makar stated, not realizing that he and Ria had been left alone in the fading quiet of the foyer.

"Thank you, Maighstir Makar," Ria acknowledged with a smile that reached her eyes. Where Flur had knelt, Ria approached instead with a steady, graceful stride. Rising on her toes, she kissed his cheek, soft, warm, carrying the faint scent of lavender and desert wind. "I know that you'll take great care of your people. Garion would be proud."

The old general blinked, his throat tightening. The distant crackle of a fire echoed faintly from another room. "Thank you for saying so, Ria. I can't help but wonder what he'd think about you and Rhyslin."

Ria reached up and cupped his cheek. Her fingers were cool, calloused from travel. "Just what you thought. He'd want me to be happy, and he'd get a laugh out of it being Rhyslin."
A knowing smile crossed her lips. "Can you recall how many times Rhyslin turned down a night in the arms of one of my ladies in waiting?"

"He'd find it downright funny," Makar admitted, his chuckle low and fond. "He'd be the first to congratulate Rhyslin." He sighed softly, the sound carrying the weight of years. "What were you looking for when you three put together this treaty?"

Ria gazed into the general's eyes as she thought about his question. The sunlight had shifted, catching in the motes of dust between them like drifting gold. After a moment, she explained,

"At first, I wanted a way for our people to escape the desert if they wished. Traveling and working freely in the Saorsa would help them do so." She glanced over her shoulder, realizing they were alone now.

Their footsteps echoed lightly as she started down the hallway toward the nearest sitting room, Makar falling into step beside her. "How many years do you think we'll have before the sands take over the oasis?"

"Danyion has estimated that the oasis will be no more in ten years. The sands will have buried it deep." His fingers tapped the hilt of his sword, the faint metallic rhythm echoing his unease.

"How many of our people would take the chance to move to a safer place?"

Makar tried to laugh but managed only a short, rough snort. "I know I'd be the first to leave, as would my family."

He bowed his head, scratching his nose with a calloused hand. "There are about five thousand of us, and I imagine that almost all of us would move away from those damned shifting sands."

He stopped mid-stride, the light from a nearby window cutting a long shadow across his face as a thought struck him. "Damn, I'm slow." Turning to Ria, he met her gaze fully. "It would be better to come into the Saorsa as equals than show up as beggars." He reached out, resting a hand on her shoulders. "Please forgive me for what I was thinking," he whispered, leaning forward until his brow touched hers.

"There's nothing to forgive you, old coot," Ria murmured, her breath warm between them. "Although maybe it should be Maighstir old coot."

A genuine laugh escaped him—deep, rough, and full of life. It echoed down the empty corridor like a welcome breeze after long stillness. Drawing a deep breath, he asked, "Is there land that we could buy?"

"I'd wager that there's land somewhere that we can buy," Ria said, stepping back with renewed purpose. "Just as there are those who have the funds to buy new lands." She rubbed her hands together, the gesture sharp with thought. "If not, then maybe our people can pool their money and buy a huge tract of land to build upon. We'd have to ask Maighstir Rhyslin."

"Then, let's discuss this with Rhyslin and see what he says." Makar's eyes swept the hall, as if the old draoidh might appear any moment. "Do you know where they might be?"

Ria nodded. "I do. I think they'll be just down the hall."

Together they walked toward the sound of voices, their steps measured and soft.

The golden light of the foyer dimmed behind them, replaced by the cooler glow of lamplight ahead. Somewhere deeper in the mansion, laughter drifted faintly, a reminder that even in the shadow of loss, life still found its way to endure.

The murmur of voices drifted through the open doorway as Rhyslin and Makar entered the sitting room. The scent of pipe smoke and mulled wine lingered faintly in the air, mingling with the resinous fragrance of the fire crackling in the hearth. Plush carpets muffled their boots, and the low amber light from a chandelier reflected off the polished surfaces of decanters and goblets scattered across the table.

The conversation died out as the two men crossed the threshold, and every head turned toward them.

Sloan, sprawled lazily in an armchair, lifted his chin with a grin that glinted in the firelight.

"It's about time you joined us," Sloan said, earning a quick jab in the ribs from Allanagh. "Hey, I said what everyone was thinking." He waggled a finger toward his bond, his smile unrepentant.

"I know, mo chridhe," Allanagh said as she leaned against him, her voice soft with affection. "But a look at them tells a different story." She gestured subtly toward Ria, then toward Makar.

The Bhanna blushed slightly, color blooming high on her cheeks. The flickering firelight made the faint sheen in her eyes look almost golden. She glanced up at the general, meeting his gaze for an instant before lowering her eyes, a silent exchange that said, I'll leave this to you.

Makar's shoulders sagged as though the weight of the desert had returned to them. He drew a slow, measured breath, the sound soft beneath the room's watchful quiet, and closed his eyes in silent prayer before addressing Rhyslin.

"What do you know of our people, old friend?"

Rhyslin leaned back against the thick cushions of his chair. The firelight danced across his weathered features as he spoke. "The clann an fhàsaich live on the edge of na gainmhich loisgte. The last time I was in the area, roughly seven thousand Hin I-Balanath lived in about seven communities of a thousand souls." His eyes softened, the reflection of the flames flickering in them. "The burning sands have been slowly moving toward the Abhainn Phecha."

Makar nodded, visibly impressed that the draoidh remembered such detail after so many years. "How long ago was that, if you don't mind me asking?"

"It must have been about sixty years ago," Rhyslin mused, his voice carrying a quiet reverence for time passed.

Makar drew a deep breath, his jaw tightening. "There are now only five thousand of us." His tone was heavy, each word seeming to settle in the air like falling ash. "We've lost two communities. One twenty years ago, when the burning sands buried the Almagord Oasis. We lost the second community last week when the cnoc a' Chèitein oasis fell." His voice cracked at the end, and he swayed slightly before Rowena, silent and watchful near the wall, slid a chair behind him. He sank into it with a quiet sigh of gratitude.

"It is estimated that the burning sands will bury the last oasis in another ten years, and we will be no more." The words hung over the group like smoke. Makar buried his head in his hands, his breath shuddering. "Rhyslin, my old friend," he said, lifting his face, his eyes bright with pain, "we need this treaty. We don't want to have to move here as beggars. We'd rather buy some land and set up communities. Would that be possible?"

The old draoidh nodded, his expression solemn but kind. "It is. I know of several places where you could start new communities." He leaned forward, the fire's glow outlining his silver hair. "Tell me about your communities, please."

"Each community is a thousand folk. Each is self-sufficient, having everything a small settlement needs—from farmers to townspeople."

Makar's voice steadied as he spoke of home. "They don't take up much space. We would need the material to build the new communities."

Rhyslin's eyes drifted upward, calculating silently. "A thousand people is a good-sized Freehold or a medium-sized town." Seeing the puzzled looks of the Hin I-Balanath soldiers, he added, "A Freehold is usually a good-sized manor with outlying houses, barns, a greenhouse, and fields within the walls—much like this estate." He gestured to the room around them, the polished beams and thick stone walls catching the lamplight.

"And a town?" Makar questioned. "Is it something like Trì aibhnichean daingneach?"

"Exactly like that," Rhyslin replied, smiling faintly. "A town within the walls, with farmland outside them. Either can be constructed within a month.

The council has several prepared building plans for both Freeholds and towns." His smile broadened, a spark of pride in his eyes. "Or you could design your own. It would take longer, but our planners are thorough. I have a captain turned sheriff that's in our newest town."

"Eola," Rowena murmured, her tone soft and knowing. "You're talking about Maighstir Balgair, aren't you?"

Rhyslin nodded. "Yes. That town has about two hundred people so far. It can easily hold another five hundred within its walls, and there's enough open land for farms to spread. Your people can farm, right?"

The general's booming laugh broke through the tension, a sound rich and grounding. "Of course we can. We've learned to grow crops that need little water and to raise both food and work animals."

His mirth faded into thought. "The only thing we'd have to watch out for are your dryads. It may take us time to get used to them—we've had our share of— intimate dealings with the sand walkers."

Rhyslin waved a dismissive hand, smiling. "The dryads won't be any problem. They'd love the company and would help your people find the best land for crops. They'd keep most of the pests out of your fields."

"I've never seen a dryad," Makar admitted, his voice quieter now. "I've always wanted to meet at least one."

"All you had to do was ask, old friend," Rhyslin said, eyes glinting as he closed them. The air shifted subtly, the warmth of the hearth seeming to pulse with quiet resonance. Somewhere unseen, a low hum spread through the floorboards and into the bones of the room, a sound ancient and alive, vibrating like a plucked harp string through the walls.

"What was that?" Flur sprang to her feet, eyes wide, her golden hair catching the lamplight. She looked around, startled by the unseen presence.

Ria and Rowena both blinked, their expressions softening in recognition. "Is that Foghar?" Ria asked, leaning closer to Rhyslin.

"Yes, it is," he replied, opening his eyes again, calm as ever. "She said she'll be here soon. She's in the middle of an instruction block, but when she's through, she'll bring her apprentice."

Flur rubbed her arms, gooseflesh rising on her skin. "That felt strange. Almost as if a tree was—" Her mouth formed a perfect O as realization dawned. "Oh, I see. Because she's bonded to her tree."

"Very good," Rhyslin said with quiet pride. He rose, stretching his arms toward the nearby door. "How about we move to the library? There's more room to spread out—and more chairs to sit in."

The group began to rise, the soft rustle of clothing and the low murmur of voices filling the air again.

As they moved toward the hall, the faint hum of the dryad's presence lingered, blending with the warm light of the hearth—an echo of something vast and living beyond the walls. The scent of cedar and smoke followed them into the corridor, carrying the promise of new beginnings.

Chapter Five

The Gathering of Fell Eggs

The chamber was dim, lit only by the restless flicker of green-blue flames burning in obsidian sconces. Incense hung thick in the air, threaded with the metallic tang of blood. Shadows clung to the stone like old secrets, whispering softly at the edges of hearing. Iktomi lounged at the far end of the long stone table, at ease, the dark threads of his power humming faintly through the walls like tension in a web.

"You've sent the skellet-drache and todesritter, where and for what?"

Saldren Halber-Drache narrowed his eyes in disbelief, his voice echoing harshly against the stone before the gloom swallowed it.

Iktomi leaned forward, slow and deliberate. Firelight slid across the spider tattoo between his eyes, making it seem to stir.

"Not that I require your permission to do anything, Saldren," he said calmly. "I sent my servants to my old plane to gather some of my pets and bring them to this world."

The half-drake's scales caught the light as he shook his head, irritation telegraphed in the snap of his tail. His gaze shifted toward the woman seated beside Iktomi. "Do you think this is a good idea?"

Brigid shrugged, silver bangles chiming faintly as her hand rested against her rounded belly.

"I don't, but Lord Iktomi didn't ask me for permission."

Her attention returned to Saldren, eyes lingering on the faint glimmer of wings behind his shoulders.

Saldren ground his teeth, the sound sharp in the stillness.

"If you are going to cause random acts of chaos, you could at least let me know."

The flames along the wall fluttered at the edge of Iktomi's awareness.

Iktomi's faint smile thinned. The air around him cooled as his eyes darkened, depth folding inward until light failed to linger there.

"And why should I, a god, tell you anything?"

The words carried softly, drawn tight as silk under strain.

The space between them thickened. Iktomi felt it settle, the way a room does when it remembers fear.

Saldren's wings flexed, scaled edges rasping faintly against stone.

"Because, in your name, I'm juggling an army of malcontents, two Ogren tribes, and the entire An fheadhainn a thuit Tribe. That's several thousand people who will switch their allegiance to you."

He leaned forward.

"But they won't if you don't start taking this seriously."

Iktomi rose.

The shadows followed him as he stood, drawn close, obedient. Each step carried him nearer, unhurried, his presence bending the space between heartbeats. His smile did not waver as he closed the distance.

Brigid's chair scraped softly as she shifted back from the table.

Iktomi stopped just short of Saldren, his voice level, unraised, absolute.

"Do you think it's a good idea to yell at me?" Iktomi asked, his tone deceptively calm. "I may have just woken up, and I may not be at full strength, but I guarantee that I am strong enough to make you suffer." He reached out and poked the half-drake in the chest, feeling the prickle of resistance beneath his fingertip as unseen energy crackled outward.

Saldren snapped at his finger on instinct, teeth flashing like a cornered beast's. Iktomi didn't bother to brace. The retaliation answered itself—an invisible force hurled the half-drake across the chamber. Stone cracked thunderously as Saldren struck the wall, dust and fragments cascading to the floor in a lazy shimmer of torchlight.

Iktomi strolled after him, unhurried, bare feet silent against the black stone. He bent, fingers closing around Saldren's throat, and lifted him with effortless ease. The half-drake's claws scraped uselessly at his wrist, tail lashing, the movements frantic and unfocused.

"You may be a half-drake, but I am a god," Iktomi whispered, letting the words resonate inside bone and breath alike. He released him without ceremony. Saldren hit the floor hard, the sound echoing off the walls. "I don't mind you questioning me, but once I've answered, don't ever argue with me."

Iktomi watched him struggle upright, noting the stiffness in his movements, the way his chest dragged air back into itself. The fire still burned in the half-drake's eyes. Good. Broken servants were useless.

"Yes, yes," Iktomi murmured, circling him with a predator's patience. "Feel the anger. Let it guide you." He touched the same place on Saldren's chest again. This time, he fed energy instead of pain.

Chaos pulsed outward. Torches flared blue-white. Bruises faded, scales knitting smooth beneath the glow. "That's right, don't surrender," he continued softly. "Show me that strength that made you what you are."

Saldren's growl rolled low and rough, vibrating the stone. He straightened, gaze burning as he looked down at Iktomi. "We can question your decisions?" Disbelief edged his voice—along with something sharper, more dangerous. "What kind of god are you?"

Iktomi laughed, the sound bright and cutting, sharp enough to make the flames gutter. "The kind of god who doesn't want blind obedience. I want obedience, but I want my followers to use their brains." He reached up and patted Saldren's shoulder, leaving his hand there just long enough to remind him who allowed this defiance.

"What are the followers of the Mother like? Or the followers of the Guardian, or the Dreamer, or even the Feathered Serpent? Do they question their god or goddess? Do they blindly obey?"

"Of course not," Brigid said from the side. Her voice was steady, though her hands still guarded her womb. "Very few people blindly follow anybody. That's why the people who supported me haven't sold me out." She smiled faintly. "They think I'll be back, and if I return to Eola, they'll covertly lend assistance."

Iktomi inclined his head, eyes gleaming with approval. "Do you think blind obedience will work with Ogres or An fheadhainn a thuit?" He let the question linger, watching it settle. "They've already betrayed one god so far."

The firelight caught in Saldren's silver scales as he frowned, weighing the words. Iktomi felt the hesitation ripple through him—resistance thinning, not breaking. Not yet.

"Blind obedience will not work with this army," the half-drake said at last, his voice stripped of its earlier heat. "But I am unsure what will. What do you suggest?"

Iktomi chuckled, low and indulgent. Mortals always reached this point eventually, when force failed and imagination ran dry. "Tell them what they want to hear. Tell the Orcan and Ogren they'll get what they want if they worship me."

The spider tattoo between his eyes pulsed, warm and pleased.

"Tell the An fheadhainn a thuit that they can enslave their kin again if that's what they wish. Promise them the sky and the moon. Promises are easy." He smiled. "Belief is the hard part."

Saldren blinked. Iktomi tasted the conflict in him—admiration fouled with revulsion. The half-drake's gaze flicked toward Brigid, as if seeking something steady.

"What about me?" Saldren asked.

Iktomi tilted his head, studying him. "What do you want?" His voice softened, coaxing. "What is your heart's desire?"

The answer came through clenched teeth. "I want respect from my enemies. I want to see these forests burn. I want to kill dryads. I want the world to acknowledge my power."

Iktomi smiled wider.

"Is that all?" he murmured. "You may have all that and more as my right hand. Play your cards well, and you may rule as much of this world as you dare to take."

The change in Saldren was immediate. Iktomi watched resolve settle over him like cooling iron. Slowly, deliberately, the half-drake knelt, clawed hand pressing to the stone floor. The air thickened as belief took root—ozone, dust, devotion.

Iktomi closed his eyes and drank.

He had missed this.

Followers calling on his name. Offering themselves without being asked. When he opened his eyes again, golden motes swirled through the blackness of them, embers caught in a storm.

"Gather your generals," he said. "I will help you shape your plans. The more who worship me, the stronger we become."

"Yes, ancient one," Saldren whispered, forehead nearly touching the floor.

The silence that followed pleased Iktomi. The temple listened. The shadows leaned closer.

Black stone walls rose around him, drinking in the light. Strange symbols pulsed along the floor, slow and patient, mirroring the rhythm of his power. He seated himself upon the obsidian throne, volcanic glass seamless and absolute beneath him. Behind, four braziers burned with pale violet flame, their smoke curling upward and vanishing before it reached the vaulted ceiling.

Soon, he thought. Soon, Nan Diathan would have no choice but to notice him.

Within the hour, priestesses gathered and sang his praises, their voices rising and falling in practiced devotion. Iktomi let the sound wash over him, then tuned it out entirely. Their belief was serviceable. Nothing more.

His fingers tapped once against the arm of the throne.

"What do you think?" he asked mildly.

Brigid sat nearby on a lesser throne, dark marble veined with crimson. Iktomi watched her stiffen before she answered.

"I'm not a priestess," she said carefully.

"You are," he replied. "You simply refuse the name." His gaze lingered on her. "When you accept your place, my power will answer you more readily."

She shifted, hands drawn protectively inward. Iktomi noted the tension, the way her breathing betrayed her even when her words did not.

"I already draw on your power," she said. "You granted me that when I freed you."

"So I did," he agreed, pleased. "And how does it feel?"

She did not answer at once. Iktomi watched the faint stir beneath her skin, the subtle reaction that never escaped him. The spark he had placed within her responded to his presence, warm and restless.

He smiled.

The braziers flared briefly, illuminating sigils along the walls that twisted and adjusted themselves to his mood. Somewhere far off, a slow drum began to beat, deep and steady, echoing like a second heart.

The temple settled into stillness again, violet fire crackling softly as Iktomi leaned back upon his throne—patient, satisfied, and growing stronger by the breath.

———————— ◆ ◆ ◆ ————————

The wind moaned low through the cracked towers of the necropolis, carrying the dust of centuries across Despair's armor. He stood at the edge of the shattered courtyard while bone spires clawed at the ashen sky, their surfaces etched with runes whose meanings had long since rotted away.

Beside him, the Skelletdrache unfurled its skeletal wings. Soot drifted from its ribs with each measured stretch, the joints creaking like timbers left too long in salt air. Emberlight burned faintly in the hollow sockets of its skull as it tested the span of its wings.

[Did the Ancient One say where we are going?] The thought brushed Despair's mind like a cold wind through a crypt.

He adjusted the dark plates of his armor, tightening the straps until they bit snugly against the cold shell of his form. His gauntlets rasped softly as he worked. "He said discord would reveal the path," Despair replied, lifting his gaze to the towering creature. "And that we were to bring back eggs."

The Skelletdrache's tail coiled through the dust behind it, stirring ash into slow spirals.

[Discord, eh? That should be interesting. How many?]

"A half dozen," Despair said. "Enough to create chaos."

Silence followed. Wind threaded through the dragon's empty ribs, whispering like breath through bones. Then came a low rumble that vibrated through the stone beneath Despair's boots.

[Are you ready?]

Despair lowered his visor. The metallic snap rang sharp in the stillness. He climbed the dragon's spine, settling into place between its skeletal wings. "I'm ready, old friend," he said. "Let's do this."

The Skelletdrache launched.

Its vast wings beat once, twice, sending black dust spiraling upward and scattering the faint blue ghostfires that burned in the streets below. The necropolis fell away beneath them as they climbed, circling the city of the dead twice before turning east.

From above, the world was a maze of tombs and broken halls, lit by flames that gave no warmth. As they rode the thinning air, distant chanting drifted up from unseen catacombs, echoes swallowed by height and wind.

[What do these eggs look like?]

The question came as they left the necropolis behind.

"They're leathery," Despair replied, leaning forward as the wind hissed past his helm. "About knee-high. Four-fold petals on top."

A pause. Then—

[Why does that sound familiar?]

Before Despair could answer, the air ahead of them rippled.

Reality split.

The tear opened like a wound in the sky, edges shimmering with distortion. Without hesitation, the Skelletdrache passed through.

The world inverted.

Cold gray gave way to violent color and sound. Pandemonium stretched before them—vast and crushingly close all at once. Violet lightning tore upward into the churning heavens. Rivers of molten glass flowed through floating islands of stone that drifted like embers through a furnace.

"I will never get used to that," Despair muttered, scanning the warped sky. Wind shifted direction without warning, and the horizon refused to stay where it belonged. "Let's find the eggs and get out."

The dragon circled once, its bones gleaming beneath the strange light, then angled toward a jagged range of black mountains rising ahead.

[Discord should be just beyond those peaks.]

They climbed. Wingbeats sent frost and ash tumbling from the dragon's frame as they cleared the highest ridge by inches. The air thinned, sharp with ozone and burning stone.

Below them, mist and shadow churned in a wide valley. For hours they rode the winds, weaving above clouds that glowed faintly from fires hidden beneath.

At last, the mountains fell away.

Plains stretched before them—flat, gray, shimmering with unnatural heat. The horizon pulsed faintly, as though the land itself breathed.

"Where would he hide them?" Despair asked, scanning the wasteland.

The Skelletdrache dipped lower. Through the haze, an ancient structure emerged—an obsidian monolith half-swallowed by fog. Its towers leaned like broken teeth, veins of red light glowing faintly through the cracked stone.

[Perhaps there.]

Unease crept into the thought.

Despair studied the temple as they descended, watching how the mist clung to it, curling and shifting like something alive. "It's as good a place as any."

The dragon folded its wings and dropped.

Fog swallowed them.

The air grew colder, heavier with each heartbeat. Sound dulled, light dimmed, and the world narrowed to stone, mist, and the promise of chaos waiting below.

✦ ✦ ✦

The Skellet-Drache circled once, its bones gleaming faintly in the red-tinged mist that hung over the ancient temple. Below, the platform jutted out from the structure's heart like a slab of dark obsidian, its surface slick with centuries of grime and shadow. Cracks webbed through the stone, and streams of faint green light pulsed beneath, like veins carrying some corrupted lifeblood.

"Will that platform hold you?" Despair asked as the Skellet-Drache dipped lower, the beat of its skeletal wings scattering the mist.

[It looks sturdy enough,] Death replied, voice reverberating through Despair's mind like a chorus of hollow bells.

[You might want to get ready to jump, just in case it's not as sturdy as I think.]

On the next pass, the massive draconic frame descended. Its claws scraped against the stone with a sound like grinding iron. The eighty-foot-long creature settled carefully, the entire platform shuddering under its weight. When it stilled, Despair hopped down, the impact of his metal boots echoing against the hollow expanse.

He ducked under one curved wing, the air around him thick with the scent of old dust and burnt resin.

[Go, get the eggs. I'll hop up to the top of the temple and wait for you.]

"As you wish," Despair said, his voice flat beneath his helm. He started down the platform toward the half-open doorway at the far end.

The ancient armor he wore, blackened by fire and pitted with corrosion, rattled faintly as he moved.

The doorway yawned before him, a wound in the temple's face. Beyond it, darkness swallowed everything. As he stepped through, the silence changed. What had been only still air became a symphony of soft groans, rattling chains, and the low, endless murmur of unseen voices.

The first chamber was slick with blood, though he couldn't tell if it was fresh or the stain of ages. Skeletons hung from the ceiling like macabre wind chimes, swaying slightly in a current he could not feel.

In the next space, the walls dissolved into smoke, and hooded shapes sat rocking slowly, their faces hidden beneath deep cowls. They whispered in tongues he didn't recognize, broken prayers, perhaps, or curses too old for memory.

A pale, bloated face drifted out of the gloom, brushing against his path. He stopped, tilting his head as the visage wavered, and melted into that of a wan, sorrowful woman before dissipating. The air carried the faint scent of rot and incense.

Despair stepped on something soft that gave way with a wet crunch. He didn't look down. Whatever it had been, it was part of the temple now.

Reaching out with his undead senses, he felt the pulse of chaotic energy running through the stone, through the walls, pure, unfiltered entropy. A flicker of grim amusement ghosted through him. If this was the worst the temple could muster, he had little to fear.

At the next pool of flickering light, a figure stepped forward. It wore a tattered robe that might once have been red, now the color of dried blood. It was man-shaped, but wrong, its arms ended not in hands but jagged claws. Under the cowl, something chittered and shifted. The sound was insectile, alien.

When it sniffed the air and caught the scent of death upon him, it froze. Slowly, the creature bent in a low bow and retreated into the dark.

[What's going on in there?] Death's voice echoed distantly from the rooftop.

[Just the usual, beings of chaos determining the pecking order,] Despair replied, his tone edged with irony. [So far, I appear to be the top predator present.]

A low rumble of amusement rolled back through their shared link before the dragon fell silent again.

Despair pressed on, the glow of his eyes cutting through the dark like lantern flame. Turning slightly to his left, he followed the pull of energy toward a deeper shadow where an altar rose from the gloom.

Before he could step into the open, a figure lurched from the dark, a corpse, skin gray-green and wet, carrying a bound woman draped over one shoulder. The smell of decay was thick enough to taste.

The wight stopped before him and raised one putrefying hand. Despair stood motionless, wondering if his cursed armor would deflect the creature's touch. The hand stopped inches from his breastplate. The corpse snarled, then stepped back, clutching the limp body closer, as if to protect its claim.

"Go your way, creature. I don't want your prize."

The wight hissed but obeyed, shuffling to the altar. It laid the woman's spirit down upon the black stone. For a moment, nothing happened.

Then, with a sound like tearing silk, the spirit screamed, its body twisting into light as it was drawn into the altar.

White flames flared at each corner, flickering like the tongues of judgment.

"Another innocent for the eternal flame," came a voice behind him, smooth and almost amused.

Despair turned, the eerie blue-white glow of his eyes falling upon a green-skinned man draped in bloodstained robes. Slightly pointed ears peeked from beneath his hood.

"An fheadhainn a thuit, here?" Despair asked, the edge in his tone cutting through the gloom.

The stranger smiled faintly. "A fallen one? Not exactly. I am Claigeann, a priest of the chaos god." He inclined his head. "Might you be Despair?"

If he had eyebrows, they'd be raised. The death knight muttered. "That is what I am called, yes."

Claigeann's thin smile deepened. "Did you arrive with a companion named Death?"

Despair's gauntleted hand drifted toward the hilt of his broadsword. [I think we were expected,] he sent silently.

[Ohmm, are you sure?]

[Fairly sure, yes. There's a priest here who knows my name and yours.]

Death's tone was thoughtful. [Iktomi did send us here—to his temple. It's possible these people expected us. Confirm it, then see if they have the eggs.]

[Very well,] Despair replied, lowering his hand. "Yes," he said aloud, "Death is here."

Claigeann nodded approvingly. "Would you believe me if I told you your coming was foretold?"

"Foretold, by who?"

"By Lord Iktomi, of course." The priest gestured deeper into the temple. "Would you come with me? I have something to show you."

"I will go with you," Despair warned, eyes flaring bright as witchlight. "But if you seek to betray me, I will kill you."

Claigeann dipped his head in a half-bow and turned. "Almost a thousand years ago, it was prophesied that, in the fullness of time, Lord Iktomi would escape his captivity and send a death knight and a skeletal dragon to gather his eggs to take to a new world."

Despair followed in silence, his footsteps ringing hollow against the copper-veined floor. The air grew thicker, heavy with heat and the scent of molten metal. The walls were alive with movement, runes crawling like insects across the surface.

"Here we are," Claigeann said, halting before a great wall covered in glowing script.

Despair scanned the runes from right to left, their shifting light reflected in the depths of his helm. [It seems legitimate, my friend. A written prophecy describes Iktomi's escape from prison, his appearance in another world, and a death knight and skeletal dragon who come to gather some eggs.]

[Interesting,] Death murmured across the link. [If we are expected, let's gather these eggs and return to Crann na Beatha.]

[I'm on my way.] Despair turned to Claigeann. "Do you know where these eggs are stored?"

"Of course," the priest replied, gesturing toward a shadowed archway. "They are in the Nesting Chamber."

"Lead on, Horatio," Despair said, his tone dry with irony.

Claigeann blinked at the unfamiliar reference but said nothing. Together they descended a narrow hall that smelled of copper and old smoke until they reached a pair of massive doors, each cast from burnished metal engraved with flowing shapes that writhed when the torchlight hit them.

Despair paused to study the pictographs, tracing their lines with a gauntleted finger. His helm tilted slightly. "Queen Mother Egg Layer? What is inside that chamber?" His hand returned to his sword.

"The Queen Mother Egg Layer," Claigeann replied softly. "She's hard to describe. You'll have to see her for yourself." He laid one green hand upon the metal. "She will appear strange, so don't attack her—or her eggs."

The doors shuddered faintly beneath his touch, as if something vast stirred on the other side. A low, wet sound echoed beyond the threshold, and the air grew warmer, thick with the scent of musk and decay.

Despair's hand stayed on his sword hilt, but he nodded once. "Very well. Open it."

"Where did she come from?" Despair asked.

Claigeann swayed slightly, his voice slipping into a reverent cadence as he recited, the coppery light from the runes rippling over his face. The air in the chamber was thick with heat and the heavy scent of resin and decay. "Her egg fell from beyond the stars; from it, she hatched." His tone was almost liturgical, as if he were speaking of a saint rather than a monster. "She and her children rampaged across Pandemonium, using the souls as nestings for other eggs. A thousand years ago, Iktomi and his followers chased her down and caged her here in the temple. From there, he changed her children from the monsters, turning them into Suffron."

The priest's hand trembled as he put his weight against the door. The copper hinges groaned, scraping against stone as it swung open. A rush of warm, damp air met them, alive with a faint clicking and the subtle hiss of shifting membranes.

Despair followed Claigeann into the chamber, his boots clanging against the slick stone floor. The air pulsed faintly, rhythmic, as though the entire room were breathing. Across the floor lay hundreds of objects that could only be called eggs, thick-shelled and glistening, their leathery surfaces glimmering faintly with reflected torchlight. Each stood about two feet tall, slick with a sheen that looked wet even in the dimness.

Fine strands of mist coiled above them, carrying a low, organic heat that smelled faintly of iron and musk.

He leaned forward, the steel plates of his armor creaking as he examined the nearest egg. The leathery surface quivered at his proximity, the four folded ridges at its crown twitching like petals sensing the sun.

"Beware," Claigeann warned softly, his voice thin in the humid dark. "The young are drawn to heat and attack without warning."

Despair said nothing, though he wondered what "young" meant in a place like this. His gauntleted hand brushed the side of the nearest egg, and the surface was warm, too warm, pulsing faintly like a heartbeat.

He barely had time to register the motion before the crown split open with a wet hiss. Something small and fast launched at his face.

Instinct guided his movement; his arm snapped up, catching the creature mid-leap.

It writhed in his grip, the sound of slick flesh against metal echoing faintly. The main body was no wider than his hand, ringed by eight spindly limbs that flexed and clawed for purchase. Two sagging sacs pulsed beneath its underside, and a long tail coiled down his wrist, strong enough to dent his armor. Its body was slick and pale, veined faintly with light. When he turned his wrist, the creature hissed, then spat a bead of milky fluid that hissed where it struck the stone.

"This is a youngling?" he asked, tightening his grip slightly as it struggled.

"Not exactly," Claigeann said, edging closer. "It's more of a secondary egg layer, only that it implants its genetic material into a host."

A deeper sound reverberated through the chamber, a drawn-out, resonant hiss that rolled through the air like a growl from the bones of the world. Dust fell from the vaulted ceiling.

Ignoring the writhing creature, Despair looked up, and froze.

From the shadows above the far wall descended a shape vast enough to make the air tremble. The creature unfurled itself from the darkness, its movements slow, deliberate, predatory. She was at least fifteen feet tall, with a long, segmented body that shimmered like blackened chitin.

The flat carapace that crowned her head caught the red light from the torches and reflected it in dull, bloody hues. Her body stretched twenty feet from head to tail, ending in a serrated blade that rasped against the stone with each motion. Two sets of arms flexed, one large and muscular, the other small and delicate, ending in claws fine as needles.

Despair stared, his helm reflecting her motionless gaze. "By the gods of darkness, what is that?"

The Queen hissed again, her head tilting as she inspected the small creature in his hand. Beneath her carapace, inner membranes flickered with dim bioluminescence, patterns of light that pulsed like language.

"That is the Queen Mother Egg Layer," Claigeann said with a strange pride.

"She's beautiful," Despair murmured, amusement flickering in his hollow eyes. "Death would find her fascinating."

The creature's tail spiraled downward, gliding through the air until it pointed directly at the struggling hatchling in his hand.

"Is she intelligent?" he asked quietly.

"Yes, she is," Claigeann replied. "She would like you to release her child and not hurt it."

Despair regarded the creature for a moment longer, then slowly raised his arm. The air hummed faintly as the Queen lowered her tail to meet the tiny thing.

The hatchling froze, its claws loosening as it reached out.

When Despair released it, it scuttled upward along the Queen's body, disappearing beneath the overhanging plate of her carapace.

The Queen's eyes, or what passed for them, shifted from Despair to Claigeann. She hissed, the sound softer now, as though forming a question.

Claigeann crossed his arms over his chest and bowed deeply. "Chaos Master Iktomi requires six of your eggs. Your children will create chaos where he wills it."

At Iktomi's name, the great creature's tail rippled with recognition. Her hiss dropped in pitch, almost mournful, before she slowly indicated six eggs with a sweep of her tail.

Claigeann stepped forward, tracing sigils in the air with long, green-stained fingers. The chosen eggs shrank slightly, their leathery shells tightening as faint runes burned across their surfaces. The smell of scorched resin filled the room. When the spell finished, each egg fit neatly into a thick leather rucksack lined with soft padding. He lifted the pack carefully and offered it to Despair. "Six eggs for our honored guest. May they serve chaos well."

"May they serve Chaos," Despair echoed, shouldering the pack. He inclined his helm toward the Queen. "Farewell, beautiful creature." As he turned and retraced his steps, the hiss of the Queen followed him, a low, rhythmic pulse that echoed like breath through the corridor.

Outside the chamber's threshold, the air was cooler, though it still reeked faintly of musk and burnt air. "You mentioned that Iktomi changed the young. In which way?" he asked as they walked.

"When the young come into the world," Claigeann explained, "they look like shadows. Their arms are longer than their bodies. They could just as well be wings of shadow dotted with spiraling light.

Where the old creatures gathered victims to implant, the Suffron hunts down those suffering and devours their spirits."

Despair paused mid-step, the faint blue glow of his eyes flaring. "If they devour souls, that will strip the world of rebirth. A' Mathair won't know what hit her."

He reached out with his mind, his voice echoing along the tether of the bond. [I am on my way back. I've got the eggs.] He sent the image of the Queen Mother shimmering behind his eyes. [You should see the Queen that laid these eggs. She's beautiful.]

The response came as a low hum of satisfaction through the link, a sound like thunder in a distant crypt.

Chapter Six

The Lesson by the Library Lamp

The hallway still held the hush of dawn when Rana stepped from her room, stifling a yawn behind one hand. Cool air drifted through the stone corridor, scented faintly of cedar polish and parchment, a reminder that the tower never fully slept, only dreamed between its inhabitants' footsteps. She padded softly toward the library, her sandals whispering over the tiled floor, the sound small against the tall silence of the place. It was Rhyslin's day to teach her again, and despite her fatigue, she found herself looking forward to it.

Halfway down the hall, a tall mirror caught her reflection. She stopped, studying the pale face that looked back, soft features framed by unruly curls and shadowed eyes.

The dark circles made her look older, more fragile. Something had stirred her awake in the night, a heaviness that seemed to press through her dreams, leaving her sleepless long after it had passed. With a sigh, she dabbed at the dark smudges beneath her eyes, knowing it would make little difference.

Her fingers lifted to her hair, tugging at a curl before letting it fall back in place. She smoothed the folds of her skirt and regarded the outfit she had chosen: a deep blue skirt and a blouse of blue-green, the faintest shimmer of seafoam in the morning light. Rhyslin refused to claim "house colors," yet all who served him instinctively gravitated to that tranquil palette. She wondered if he noticed such things. She hoped, perhaps, that he did.

Rana turned sideways, checking the back of her outfit, and tugged at a wrinkle that wasn't really there. Her sandals felt wrong, too stiff, too formal, and she missed the comfort of her moccasins. Still, she wanted to look the part of a student Rhyslin could be proud of. Satisfied at last, or at least resigned, she continued on.

The library was still and golden in the slanting light of early morning. Dust motes floated through the air like drifting stars, and the scent of old leather and ink hung heavy and comforting. Rana made her way past the high shelves until she reached the settee near the great window and curled herself into it, a history tome open on her knees. The world narrowed to the sound of her breathing and the soft rustle of paper.

Time passed without her noticing. The tower seemed to wake around her in stages—footsteps far below, the faint hum beneath the stones that told her magic was stirring again.

She sensed him before she heard him.

A presence at the edge of the room, careful, familiar.

Rana lifted her head as Rhyslin ascended the gallery stairs, his boots barely creaking against the wood. He moved as though the silence mattered. A faint pulse of light flared as he coaxed a dormant orb awake, just bright enough to cut the shadows. He crossed the room, passing desks she knew by heart, until his gaze found her curled into the corner like a half-wakeful cat.

"Good morning, mo phrìseil," he said gently as he settled beside her. "Did you sleep well?"

"Well," Rana began, rubbing at her eyes, "not really." She covered a yawn with one hand. "Something woke me up in the middle of the night, and I couldn't get back to sleep." She hesitated, then looked at him more closely. "Didn't you feel it?"

His eyebrow lifted slightly.

"What did you feel?" he asked.

Rana marked her place and closed the book with care. "Do you remember when we faced off with that Skellet-Drache?" When he nodded, a shiver ran through her. "It felt like that—only farther away. Over the mountains. Like it was circling, and then it went away."

"Yes," Rhyslin said quietly. "I felt that as well."

Relief and unease tangled in her chest. "I couldn't get back to sleep," she admitted. "I kept wondering where it went. And if it was coming for us."

He leaned back, and the quiet he chose made her chest tighten. "I had the same thought," he said at last. "And I sincerely hope not. It would take more than I have here to defeat a Skellet-Drache."

Rana swallowed. "What about the Todesritter?"

"If he doesn't have the Skellet-Drache with him, I could probably defeat him," Rhyslin said slowly. "It depends on how powerful he was while alive." His mouth tightened. "If it's both of them..."

He sighed.

"Then I don't know if I would make it. If Marcus and Rembran were here, we might come out alive—but it would be close."

Rana folded her hands together in her lap, the golden quiet of the library suddenly fragile around them.

Rana looked down, the words stinging more than she expected. "I'd have to run," she murmured, bitterness curling beneath her breath.

His arm came around her shoulders, warm and steady. "I'd probably do the same," he said quietly. "It's not cowardice to live another day."

She turned toward him, disbelief flashing hot through her fatigue. "You would run?"

Rhyslin met her gaze, calm as ever. "We didn't fight during the first encounter, and we had more firepower than I've got here." His voice softened. "Like then, I would try to avoid an outright fight. You, Flur, Ria, and Rowena are too important to me."

The words landed heavier than she expected. Too important. She swallowed, disappointed despite herself.

"Do you remember what I told you about Skellet-Draches and how they are made?" he asked.

She frowned, turning the thought over. Then she nodded slowly as understanding crept in.

"How powerful are Skellet-Draches and Todesritter?" she asked.

"A Skellet-Drache has more raw power than I do, and it doesn't have to worry about burning out. Its unlife is its power," he explained.

Then, as if changing course, "I forgot to ask—what did you think about the Ciad-Fhir?"

Rana hesitated. "They are scary. When that one released his prana, I fell to my knees and couldn't get back up." A shiver traced her spine. "I can't believe Momma thought you were one of them." She glanced up at him, cheeks warming. "You're not, are you?"

He rubbed his chin, considering. "No. I don't think so. The best I can figure is that I'm born of the weave."

She tilted her head, studying him. "How were you able to resist their spiritual pressure?"

"Apparently, I'm close enough to Ciad-Fhir to ignore that little problem," he said, a faint grin touching his mouth.

Curiosity stirred, pushing aside her fatigue. She leaned forward. "Can you, you know—" She trailed off, heat flooding her face. "Make babies?"

He waited until the embarrassment finished burning before answering. "We will find out."

She stared at him, half-scandalized.

"If A' Mathair is willing," he added lightly, "maybe Flur or Ria will bear a child."

Rana caught her breath. "What about Rowena?"

"Only time will tell," he said. "Tiene women easily bear children with compatible men."

She looked away, heart pounding. The way he spoke of life—plainly, without ceremony—left her unsteady. She forced herself back to what mattered. "How was I able to sense the Skelettdrache? You said something about being attuned to nature, but I don't understand."

Rhyslin studied her for a long moment, his gaze thoughtful.

"Certain members of all races have an affinity for the natural world," he said at last, drawing a small circle on the table with his fingertip. "I think you might be one of them."

Her mouth formed a small O. "Me, a draoidh?" she breathed. "Are you sure?"

"I am," he said simply. "You sensed the Skellet-Drache before most of the crew. That was not chance."

The room seemed to tilt. She stepped back, blinking. "I—I don't..."

"I would like you to consider that you could one day be a draoidh."

The weight of it crashed over her. Her pulse raced, her gaze darting toward the door. "I—I don't..."

"Hey." His hand reached out, steadying her. "Calm down. You don't have to decide right now."

Her chest caved in. She crossed the space before she understood she'd moved, folding into him like she'd been holding herself upright on borrowed strength. The scent of parchment, oil, and pine resin wrapped around her. His hand hesitated—just for a heartbeat—then settled, tracing slow, grounding lines down her back.

"It's okay," he murmured. "You don't have to decide right now. We've got time." His voice dropped softer still. "A lifetime, if I can help it."

"I'm sorry," she sobbed. "Please don't be mad."

"I'm not mad, Rana," he whispered. "I want you to be happy."

She stayed there until the shaking eased.

Then his voice gentled again. "What did you learn at Marcus' yesterday?"

She sniffed, muffled against his shirt. "Where you learned to cheat."

She sat up, pushing back just enough to see his face. Dust motes drifted through the amber lamplight. "I almost beat him, but he used a coiled vine to beat me."

"Is that all you learned?"

She hesitated, then reached up, cautiously cupping his cheek. The faint roughness of stubble brushed her fingertips. "I learned I can never hope to defeat a man in a fair fight. If I want to come out ahead, I must be sneaky," she said. "Or I have to run away."

The words tasted bitter. She didn't want to keep running. She still dreamed of standing her ground.

"Sneaky?" Rhyslin raised an eyebrow. "I would rather you be smart enough to avoid a fight you can't win than charge headlong into every fight."

The distraught young spell-blade looked into his eyes. The lamplight caught the gold flecks in his irises, steady and unjudging.

"Smart? I don't understand?"

Rhyslin sighed, the sound carrying both patience and a quiet ache he hadn't meant to reveal. The air smelled faintly of old parchment, candlewax, and citrus oil from the shelves He let the silence stretch, measuring not her stubbornness, but the distance between what she feared and what she called courage. "Rana," he said gently, "what is your definition of bravery and courage?"

She blinked, the question striking harder than any sparring blow. Slowly, her mouth pulled into a thoughtful frown. She climbed out of his lap and began pacing the aisle between the bookcases, her sandals whispering across the worn rug. The faint crackle of the hearth filled the space she left behind.

He let the silence sit, because any easy answer would be a lie. The wood creaked softly beneath him. The sandglass beside his elbow marked time with a thin, deliberate stream of falling grains. He let the silence stretch, trusting it. This was not a question to rush.

Footsteps approached. The scent of warm bread and honeyed tea drifted in before Ria appeared in the doorway, sunlight at her back, a tray balanced easily in her hands. Morning had fully claimed the study now, pale gold light spilling through the high windows and catching dust motes in its wake.

[Good morrow, beloved,] she murmured through their bond as she set the tray on his desk and leaned down to kiss him, brief and warm.

Rhyslin returned the greeting with a soft pulse of affection and reached for a glass of chilled citrus juice. He watched Rana pace, still muttering under her breath, her brow furrowed in concentration.

[She was complaining that she'll never beat a man in a fair fight unless she cheats or runs,] he sent quietly. [So I asked her what bravery means to her.]

Ria's hands settled on his shoulders, grounding. He felt her presence steady him.

[That was about an hour ago,] he added, glancing at the sandglass. The upper bulb was nearly empty.

[In less than three weeks, she's lost to three men she respects,] he continued when Ria prompted him with a questioning stillness. [Me. Rembran. Marcus. And then she felt the Ciad-fhir's prana on top of it.]

[Have you gone easy on her?] The question carried more concern than accusation.

He took another sip of juice, cool and sharp. [I haven't gone easy on her. I can't. If Despoina is sending her dreams, something is coming.]

He watched Rana slow her pacing, then start again, frustration rolling off her in quiet waves. [But I also have to remember she's still young.]

The conflict sat heavy in his chest. He exhaled slowly. [She's the daughter I never had... and she's also a potential bond.]

Ria went very still behind him. He felt the hesitation ripple through their link before the question came.

[Have men ever bonded with their daughters?]

He felt the edge of revulsion in the thought—more at himself than at the world's rules. He answered honestly.

[Nan Diathan do not forbid it explicitly. But it's rare. Most bonds lead to intimacy, and most men balk at the thought.]

He felt her discomfort even before she shifted, before she leaned down to kiss his cheek again, gentler this time.

[Thank you for caring about her,] Ria sent, her presence already withdrawing as she straightened. Aloud, she said nothing, only smoothed her gown and turned toward the door.

Rhyslin listened to her footsteps fade down the corridor, the study settling back into quiet.

His attention returned fully to Rana.

She had stopped pacing.

The sandglass ran out.

The silence sharpened, expectant.

When Rana returned to the couch, the worn leather gave a soft sigh beneath her weight. She gazed at him for several moments, the silence filled only by the rustle of her tunic and the whisper of the fire settling in the hearth. Finally, she said, "I want to say bravery, and courage are the same, but I have a feeling that you will say they aren't."

When he nodded, she continued, her voice steadier now. "I want to say bravery is facing your fears and acting upon them, while courage is facing danger."

Rhyslin let her sit in the silence that followed. The soft crackle of the fire, the faint tang of parchment and ink, the filtered sunlight painting golden stripes across the rug—all of it seemed to listen with him. "Courage is the choice and willingness to confront agony, pain, danger, uncertainty, or intimidation, if you can avoid it." His tone was even, measured. "There are three types of courage. They are Physical Courage, Moral Courage, and Fortitude."

He saw her puzzled expression and leaned forward slightly, his shadow stretching across the table between them. "Physical courage is bravery in the face of physical pain, hardship, even death, or threat of death. Moral courage is the ability to act rightly in the face of popular opposition, shame, scandal, discouragement, or personal loss. Fortitude is physical and moral courage, with patience and perseverance added."

He paused, his gaze drifting briefly toward the window where sunlight pooled across the sill. "Bravery is also known as Valor, which is the ability to face combat and stand strong."

Rana's fingers traced the seam of her sleeve. "Have you been in battle?"

Rhyslin nodded. "Yes, many times, including recently at daingneach nan tri aibhnichean." His voice carried the weight of memory, faint smoke and blood in his tone, ghosts that never quite left.

Rana absorbed his words as she turned her eyes toward the window, watching a thin beam of light dust the shelves. "Have you ever run from combat?"

The draoidh arched his right eyebrow. "Run away once combat started, no. Avoided combat when it wasn't needed, yes."

The spell blade blinked, her hazel eyes narrowing in thought. "What's the difference between running away and avoiding combat?"

Rhyslin scratched his chin, the rasp of his fingertips against stubble sounding loud in the quiet room. When he answered, it was with care, each word deliberate. "At daingneach nan tri aibhnichean, running wasn't an option," Rhyslin said. "I remember standing there and knowing that if we withdrew, the war pack would roll straight through the village. People would be taken. Enslaved. And I'd have to live with that." "What if they had outnumbered you? What would you have done then?"

"We would have still fought," he said softly, as though repeating an old oath. "More of us would have died, but we couldn't turn our backs and let the Orcan war pack kill innocent people."

"Ah," she breathed. "And why wasn't it the same when we faced the Skellet-drache?"

"Because the Skellet-drache wasn't threatening us," Rhyslin stated firmly. His gaze grew distant, remembering the echoing winds above the ship, the shimmer of scales in the dark. "In that case, there was no reason to fight. We would have all died, and the ship would have been destroyed, all for nothing."

Rana leaned forward, curiosity replacing doubt. "What if they had attacked?" Her voice held a quiet intensity, the sound of someone who needed to understand where the line was drawn.

When he answered, his voice was tinged with sorrow. "We would have defended ourselves until we could safely withdraw." He shook his head, his eyes dimming with reflection. "Many of us would have died, and we might have lost the ship."

"Would that have been cowardice?" Rana asked carefully, her tone almost reverent.

"There is nothing wrong in trying to avoid a fight you can't win," Rhyslin whispered. His eyes met hers, steady and kind. "Cowardice is running away and leaving your companions behind once you've initiated combat." He leaned back, exhaling a breath that felt centuries old. "Avoiding a fight you don't have to fight isn't cowardice; it's good judgment." A small, careworn smile creased his lips. "Does that make sense?"

Rana nodded, though her brow furrowed. "Why do men make such a big deal out of courage and charge into battle? They make it out to be more important than life itself." Her hazel eyes caught the firelight, flaring with frustration.

Rhyslin studied her for a long moment. She had come a long way in the three weeks she'd lived under his roof, no longer the uncertain girl who had first stumbled into his care, but someone beginning to think like a woman of reason. He didn't need time to answer. "Those who haven't fought or have only fought duels see honor in fighting and charging into battle. Those who have been in battle are more cautious about fighting and know death."

She leaned closer, voice soft but urgent. "Which is more important to you?"

The question lingered in the air, heavier than any weapon. Outside, a faint wind stirred through the pines, carrying the scent of rain. Rhyslin's gaze drifted toward the window again, as if the answer might lie somewhere beyond the shifting light.

"It depends upon your mission," he stated. The morning light slanted through the tall windows of the study, pooling in soft gold along the wooden floor. Dust motes drifted lazily through the air, stirred by the faint current from the hearth. "If you are on a scouting mission, avoid battle if you can help it. Your job isn't to fight. It's to report." He paused and looked at her, his expression patient but intent. "What did Marcus say yesterday when you were almost late?"

She blinked, caught off guard. Of all the questions she expected, that wasn't one of them. "He asked me why I was late, and I told him about the Ciad-Fhir and A Mathair. When I couldn't tell him why the Ciad-Fhir were escorting A Mathair, he looked strange but said nothing." She lowered her head, the faintest tremor in her voice. "Did I do something wrong?"

"No," Rhyslin shook his head, a small smile softening his tone. "You didn't know to stay and watch." He nodded toward her, his voice the calm certainty of a teacher long accustomed to mistakes. "A scout would have stayed, gathered information, and taken that to Marcus." His lips quirked faintly. "You'll know better next time."

Rana exhaled slowly, relief easing her tense shoulders. Her gaze fell to the table between them, a simple slab of oak marked with ink stains and candle burns, and she nodded. Still, the faint flush of embarrassment colored her cheeks. She'd spent so much time training to be a spellblade that the thought of changing her approach felt impossible. Her fingers toyed with a loose thread on her sleeve. Then, a thought struck her and she cleared her throat. "Can spell blades be scouts?"

Rhyslin grinned, eyes glinting with humor. "Spell blades are unique. They can be anything they want. They can be scouts, frontline fighters, rangers, mages, and pilots. The sky is the limit."

The reassurance struck something deep in her. The tightness in her chest loosened, and her shoulders finally dropped. Seeing her relax, Rhyslin patted her knee, a small, fatherly gesture that carried more comfort than words. "You'll be fine." The old draoidh leaned back in his chair, the leather groaning softly beneath him. "What would you like to learn today?"

Rana hesitated, chewing her lower lip. "Before we start, I would like to— Can we?" She stumbled, nerves warring with determination.

"Can we switch the lessons with Maighstir Marcus and Rembran to full days? Half days are okay, but I'm fatigued by the time I get through with them, and I don't want to miss your classes."

The draoidh regarded her quietly, his silver eyes reflecting the shifting firelight. He had wondered how long she could sustain the pace, though he hadn't voiced it. "You've only been at it for two days. Why do you want to change the hours?"

Rana met his gaze steadily. "Rembran will meet me at the practice field, and that's not too far away," she said, then paused, tracing a circle on the tabletop with one fingertip. "It's four miles to Maighstir Marc's shack, so that's four miles there, four miles back, and I have a feeling that some of Maighstir Marc's lessons will be long. I don't want to miss your lessons."

Her voice carried a faint edge of pleading, but her posture remained upright, resolute.

"I understand," Rhyslin stated after a long pause. The corners of his mouth lifted slightly, proud of her resolve. "We can amend the schedule. Rembran's class can go for eight hours a day, two days a week. Marc's class can go eight hours a day, two days a week, and my classes can go eight hours a day, two days a week." His tone invited her to rise to the commitment he was offering.

Rana's face brightened. "Thank you, Maighstir Rhyslin. That would work."

"I'll tell Marcus and Rembran about the change," Rhyslin confirmed, leaning forward slightly. "What would you like to learn today?"

Rana smiled broadly, victory glowing behind her eyes. "I want to learn more about the history of the Saorsa," she said.

"Very well," Rhyslin said with a grin. The fire cracked softly, throwing amber light across his lined features. "The Saorsa is almost three hundred years old. It was conceived as a place where free men could live and work together."

Rana straightened, quill poised above her parchment. The rhythmic scratch of ink soon joined the gentle sounds of the tower. "Is it true that the oldest structure is Maighstir Marc's hunting shack?"

Rhyslin nodded. "That's correct. My tower is the second oldest structure. Marc's shack predates the Saorsa by fifty years, and my tower predates the Saorsa by five years."

"Hold on a minute," Rana said, raising her hand, brow furrowed. "Keisha said that the first stone on your tower was placed two hundred and eighty years ago."

"Keisha is right," Rhyslin admitted, chuckling quietly. "The first stone was set two hundred eighty years ago. But the tower wasn't finished until five years before the Saorsa was founded."

"Oh, okay. That makes sense." She nibbled on her fingernail, then scribbled the note down. The air smelled faintly of ink and beeswax. "Why was the Saorsa founded?" She hesitated, then met his gaze again. "The real reason. There has to be more than just the reason you gave."

Rhyslin's chuckle was low and warm. "You are right. There is another reason." He leaned back in his chair, gaze turning inward.

The light from the hearth flickered over his hands, making them seem older, heavier. "Marcus, Natolie, and

I have been citizens of almost a half-dozen small kingdoms. Kingdoms that rarely lasted more than twenty years."

"A half-dozen? Each, or all together?" Rana's quill hovered, her voice bright with curiosity. "Why did they fail?"

"Marcus and Nat were present at the fall of four kingdoms. I survived two." He raised his hand, fingers counting off memories like the beads of an old rosary. "The reasons were varied. I think Marcus and Nat survived one that fell to tyranny. I barely managed to escape one that had pissed off Ananke. Two were destroyed by internal fighting when the king died. A neighboring kingdom overran one, and one imploded when assassins killed every member of the aristocracy in three days." He paused, his voice softening.

The fire hissed quietly, filling the silence. "Each of them had promise. Each of them failed."

Rana's hand stilled over the parchment. Her throat tightened as she watched the faint sorrow shadow his expression. "Was there another?" she asked softly.

When she saw the look in his eyes, regret twisted through her. Still, she had to know.

"Yes, there was." The words came like an old wound reopening. He fell silent for a long moment, his gaze drifting toward the map that hung on the wall, a faded parchment inked with ghostly borders and names now lost to time. "It was called the March of the Oaken Shield."

He drew a slow, steady breath, as if the act of remembering cost him. "Margrave Iain Oakenshield was an able leader who had command of the frontier between the old Empire and the wildlands. The three of us had made homes there, in a land that honored law, provided defense for the people, and let them live in freedom." His voice softened, threaded with reverence. The fire popped once, the embers flaring as if in answer.

"What happened?" Rana asked, her tone hushed.

"A group of *An fheadhainn a thuit* caught him out on patrol and followed his patrol until they made camp. Once the camp was set, they waited until the dark hours of the night and wiped out the camp. After that, the March fell apart, and we left another place we'd made home." His eyes lingered on the map, as though he could still see the outline of that lost land. "After that, we set our mind to creating our own country. One that would never fall apart. From that idea was born the Saorsa."

The words hung in the air, deep and resonant. Outside, a breeze whispered against the tower stones, and the scent of pine drifted through the open window. For a long moment, neither of them spoke. Rana sat quietly, ink drying on the page, realizing that what he had given her was not only history, but a promise, the weight of memory turned to hope.

Chapter Seven

Of Blades and Shadows

The next five days were a whirlwind of motion and purpose. Rhyslin and the men worked from dawn until the stars burned high, planning for the campaign that would soon take place at the Council Hall. The manor had taken on a rhythm of quiet urgency, the shuffle of boots in corridors, the scent of parchment and wax sealing letters, the soft murmur of voices carried through open doors. Maps unfurled across long oak tables, ink pots and candle stubs marking borders and battle lines.

Rana kept to her training, moving between teachers like a soldier on patrol. One day was spent with Rembran, the ring of steel filling the morning air as she practiced using a short sword and dirk in tandem.

The next day found her with Marcus, learning the patience of the short bow—the creak of drawn string and the hiss of released arrows echoing through the training fields. When she studied with Rhyslin, they worked indoors by lamplight, her hands smudged with ink as he spoke of the old Empire that had once ruled the southern lands.

Mayana and Allanagh, when not called into counsel, spent their hours in the library, the warm scent of vellum and ink surrounding them as they pored over scrolls and tomes. Their laughter or debate drifted faintly through the quiet halls, a small reminder that even in preparation for war, life still found its voice.

Ria was the happiest she had ever been. Rhyslin's house, once filled with stillness and study, now thrummed with life.

She moved through its rooms like sunlight through leaves, planning dinners and lunches, balancing ledgers, and working alongside Flur and Rowena to refine the delicate art of managing a household that had suddenly grown twice its size. The air often smelled of fresh bread or wild herbs, and the rhythmic sound of footsteps and quiet laughter followed her wherever she went.

Rhyslin, watching her from the stairwells or the study's shadowed doorways, saw how easily she brought warmth into the house. He had half expected her to tire of the bustle, yet she seemed to thrive in it. Even the staff responded, soft-spoken, eager, smiling. Kenna, once nervous and scattered, now straightened her apron whenever Ria passed, her face brightening with pride.

For Rhyslin, any doubts about giving her free rein faded quickly. The household ran smoother under her care, and her laughter, gentle, musical, seemed to chase away the old silence that had long haunted the halls.

On one such afternoon, Ria walked alone down one of the narrow corridors. The light there was dim, the air cool with the scent of old stone and beeswax. Tapestries stirred faintly in a draft. She carried a small ledger pressed against her hip, humming softly to herself, unaware that a pair of pale eyes followed her from the shadows.

Rhyslin waited in the recess between two sconces, cloaked in stillness. He watched her pass, her steps light, her braid swinging softly against her back, and as she drew near, he reached out.

In a single, fluid motion, he stepped from the darkness and caught her around the waist, drawing her back into the shadows.

Ria tensed as the shadows closed around her, cool and heavy as mist. The faint light from the sconces dimmed, swallowed by the narrow corridor's gloom. A breath of air stirred her hair, and the whisper of cloth brushed her arm as she was drawn backward into the corner. The scent of candle smoke and stone filled her lungs.

"Rhyslin won't like it if you do anything to me." Her voice came out sharper than she intended, half warning, half plea.

The shape behind her didn't answer. Its presence loomed, heat at her back, a weight in the darkness. She tried to twist away, but the grip that held her only tightened.

The world shrank to sound and breath: a heartbeat that wasn't hers, a low rasp near her ear, the rustle of leather against cloth. Panic clawed its way up her throat.

She reached for the bond instinctively, calling for Rhyslin. The familiar thread that connected them flickered. It felt as if Rhyslin were a million leagues away. The sudden emptiness turned her stomach; the world tilted, cold and wrong.

"Who is going to tell him? You?" The words slid across her ear, intimate and mocking. "What's wrong, little bird? Can't you call him?"

The whisper made her shiver. Her breath came unevenly, the scent of iron and stone thick around her, and the darkness seemed to press closer, testing the edges of her courage.

When one of the cold hands rested on her belly, Ria clenched her eyes shut and drew ragged breaths. She would rather die than be with anyone but Rhyslin.

"You can't call him, can you?" the draoidh whispered as he teased her. "What's to stop me from making you disappear?"

The absolute lack of emotion in that voice scared her into silence. She tried to fight the person behind her, but his hold only tightened.

Where were the guards? Where was Rhyslin? Why was this happening to her?

Just as she was about to faint, the bond burst to vivid

life. Tt was like sunshine breaking the darkness and Ria sighed as she recognized Rhyslin's prana . "Oh, mo gradh, you're so —" she wanted to say *mean* but couldn't, she was just relieved that it was Rhyslin.

Feeling her collapse against him, Rhyslin nuzzled into her hair, whispering, "I didn't mean to frighten you, but I needed to see how you would react and if you were carrying a weapon."

Ria turned in his arms and snuggled against his chest. "I tried to fight, maighstir, but I couldn't get away." she whispered. "Would you have avenged me?"

"With every fiber of my being," Rhyslin promised her as he held her close.

The afternoon light slanted through the tall windows of Rhyslin's study, gilding the edges of books and the faint motes of dust that drifted in the still air.

Outside, the manor hummed with quiet life, the murmur of voices, the soft rhythm of boots on polished floors, and the muted clatter of dishes from the distant kitchen.

Ria turned her head to look up at him. "Do you think I should start carrying a poniard?" She didn't want to carry a weapon around the house, but he had just shown her that, in an instant, anything could happen to her.

Rhyslin closed his eyes, considering. The fire crackled softly behind him, its light dancing across his face. "I won't say no if you want to carry some protection." He chuckled, the sound warm and low. "Flur carries one strapped to her left thigh."

Intrigued, Ria arched an eyebrow. "How long has she been doing that?"

"I would guess sometime in the last five days," he said, and when she quirked her other brow, he continued.

"More strangers are staying here than she knows. Maybe she felt she needed the extra protection."

"Strangers?" Ria asked, surprised. "I would hardly call Makar and Sloan strangers, and I think she even came across Silas once or twice while we were living in the castle."

Rhyslin shrugged, leaning against the desk. "She knows Sloan and Makar and probably Silas. That's three out of fifteen soldiers that came here. Are you able to vouch for anyone other than Makar?" When she shook her head, he added quietly, "If I had to guess, Flur felt the same."

Ria's eyes widened as a thought struck her. "Oh, Rhyslin, what about Rana?"

"What about her?" Rhyslin inquired. "She hasn't been unarmed since she arrived. She carries her dirk everywhere." He chuckled. "Not to mention her sword."

He leaned down and kissed her softly. "Don't worry about Rana. She can take care of herself."

Ria sagged in relief, her hand resting against his chest. "Thank you, mo gradh." She reached up and caressed his cheek. "I wasn't so scared about what would happen to me as I was about what you'd think if I had to surrender to someone stronger."

"Ahh," Rhyslin nodded in understanding. "I love you, mo Ria. Nothing could ever change that." He nuzzled into her hand. Releasing her with one arm, he reached down to his belt. "Here, keep this with you until we can get you a poniard from the armory."

She looked down and saw that he held his silver dagger. The hilt gleamed faintly in the firelight, the runes etched along the blade glinting like water under the moon.

"Are you sure?" she asked, closing her hand around the sheath. When he nodded, she grinned playfully. "Would maighstir help me secret this under my skirt?"

"With the greatest of joy, my dearest," he replied, fastening the leather strap around her right thigh. The dagger rested cool against her skin, the sheath snug and balanced. He watched as she took a few careful steps, testing its weight. "Are you going to want to wear the poniard under your skirt or at your waist?"

"I'll have to think about that. I might take Flur's lead and wear it hidden under my skirt," she admitted, still adjusting to the feel of the weapon. A flicker of gratitude warmed her features as she glanced up at him, wondering how she had been so lucky to bond with him. She paused, hesitant.

"What is it?" he asked, sensing her hesitation.

She blushed faintly. "I've never learned to use a blade for anything other than cutting food," she admitted. "Can you teach me?"

She didn't expect the sly look he gave her. "Rana

could…" It was as far as he got before she shook her head.

"No, I want you to teach me how to defend myself," Ria said firmly, her tone leaving no room for argument.

"Very well," he replied with a grin. "I'm not sure how well Flur can defend herself. I might have to teach both of you."

Ria nodded, her expression softening. "I'll ask her and Rowena about it later." She kissed his cheek, the gesture light and fond, and sauntered from the room.

Her skirts brushed softly against the floor, the faint scent of lavender trailing in her wake.

The manor's halls were warm with the scent of herbs and freshly baked bread. Through open windows came the sound of birds and the distant hum of voices, ordinary peace layered over hidden tension. It took Ria nearly an hour to track down the ciad-bhanna.

When she finally found Flur, the golden-haired woman was in the nearest garden. The sunlight caught her hair like a spill of molten gold as she knelt among the spring blooms. A handful of fairy folk flitted nearby, their wings shimmering like glass in the light as they debated which flowers could be plucked without harming the bees.

"Do you have a mionaid?" Ria asked when Flur glanced up and acknowledged her.

"Always," Flur replied, pointing out flowers to her tiny helpers before sending them away with a wave.

The air shimmered faintly with dust motes as the fairy folk disappeared into the greenery. "What can I do for you?"

"Is it true that you're carrying a poniard?" Ria asked, watching her straighten and brush soil from her hands.

Flur nodded solemnly. "It is. There are too many strangers that I don't know." She rolled her eyes and shook her head with a rueful grin. "I know they are our brothers and sisters, but I don't want to take any chances."

"I understand," Ria said quietly, the memory of the dark hallway brushing the edge of her thoughts. "Rhyslin surprised me in the hallway." She explained what he had done, and Flur snorted, half amused, half exasperated.

"He did the same to me yesterday and stopped

when he felt the blade under my skirt." She laughed.

"Wouldn't you figure, the one time I want to be accosted, the blade prevented it." The sunlight danced across her face. "If I were you, I'd get a dagger and carry it."

"Rhyslin gave me his silver dagger to carry until I can find a poniard, and he said he'd teach me how to use it."

"Oh? Can I see it?" Flur's eyes lit with interest.

"Umm, sure." Ria hesitated, glancing around to be sure they were alone. She reached beneath her skirt and drew the dagger. The polished silver caught the light, bright as starlight. "I thought it would be heavier," she murmured, offering it to Flur.

The ciad-bhanna's eyes widened slightly. "It's a magic blade," she said softly. "The runes make it lighter and sharper than a normal blade."

She traced the sigils with her fingertip, then drew her own poniard from under her skirt for comparison. "He gave you a good gift. I'm kinda jealous."

Ria smiled. "Who taught you how to use it?"

Flur's grin turned fond. "Sloan. When I told

Mother I wanted to be a healer, she made sure I could defend myself—or escape anyone who captured me."

She slid her poniard back into its sheath with practiced ease. "How is it that you never learned to use one?"

Ria flushed. "I didn't go on adventures with Garion, Maya, and Allanagh. There wasn't much use for one at the castle."

Flur nodded, her blue eyes twinkling. "Makes sense. I'm surprised he didn't offer to get Rana to teach you."

Ria sighed and dropped her head into her hands, making Flur laugh. "He did, didn't he?"

Ria nodded wordlessly.

"That would be funny as Ifrinn to watch," Flur teased.

"Flur!" Ria exclaimed, mortified. "She would take great joy in torturing me."

Flur patted her shoulder affectionately. The scent of mint and crushed petals drifted between them.

Ria glanced toward the manor. "Do you think Rowena knows how to...?"

"Do I know what?" came Rowena's voice as she

approached, her dark skirts whispering over the garden path. Her raven-black hair shimmered in the sun.

"How to use a knife?" Ria asked, smiling.

"Of course I do," Rowena said easily. "The collegium taught me to defend myself before I could graduate." She reached through a slit in her skirt and drew a slender silver dagger etched with faint runes. "It's not much, but it's something." She leaned toward Ria with a knowing smirk. "Rana could teach you..."

She jumped back at Ria's glare. "Umm. I get it—not a good idea." She sheathed the dagger again, the faint rasp of metal against leather punctuating the air.

Ria sighed softly, her shoulders drooping. "Everyone but me knows how to use a knife."

"Hey, don't let it get you down," Rowena said gently. "Rhyslin will enjoy teaching you, but I didn't expect you ever to carry a weapon." She paused as the sound of bootsteps echoed faintly from the corridor beyond the archway.

Four of Sloan's men passed, their voices low, their armor creaking softly. Rowena's gaze followed them. "Yeah, too many people you don't know. I understand."

Her tone grew distant. "There'll be more at the council meeting. Many, many more."

Ria watched the men disappear, fingers tightening around the dagger's sheath. Before bonding with Rhyslin, she would have thought nothing of it. Now, a quiet unease stirred under her skin.

When the hall was empty again, Flur and Rowena exchanged a glance, sunlight catching in their eyes. Flur poked Ria's shoulder. "Why don't you want Rana to work with you?"

"Just what every mother wants—for her daughter to tell her what to do," Ria sighed. "She'd enjoy it too much." Her voice softened.

"We've just started getting along again, and I don't want to lose that closeness." She flicked her hair over her shoulder and straightened. "If you aren't going to help me, I've got things to do," she said briskly, turning back toward the house.

The garden fell quiet again save for the whisper of wind through the leaves and the laughter of the fairy folk among the blooms. Ria's footsteps faded toward the manor—measured, purposeful, carrying with them not fear, but resolve.

Chapter Eight

Raiment and Resolve

Even though Ria acted mad at her bond sisters, she really wasn't. She would rather have a stranger train her than for her daughter to have that kind of power. Still, she hurried through her remaining tasks, her hands deft but distracted. The day's hum filled the house, footsteps in distant corridors, the faint clink of crockery, the low murmur of women's voices that rose and fell like a tide. When at last her duties were done, she dried her hands on her apron and began her search for Rhyslin.

The manor was cool and still in the afternoon light. Dust motes drifted in golden shafts from high windows, and the faint scent of parchment, herbs, and old wood grew stronger as she climbed the stairs.

She found him in his study on the second floor, seated at a broad oaken desk strewn with scrolls and a single quill resting idle in the ink. His head was bowed slightly, eyes half-closed in thought. The sunlight from the tall, arched window behind him fell in ribbons across his shoulders, catching the silver strands in his hair.

He looked so peaceful that she didn't want to disturb him. For a few moments, she simply watched, the quiet rhythm of his breathing slowing her own. Then, with a soft sigh, she turned and began to leave.

She didn't get far before hearing him say, "Why don't you stay, onya."

The warmth in his voice made her pause. She looked over her shoulder and saw his eyes on her, calm, steady, the faintest smile curving his lips.

When she turned back to him, he saw the doubt in her eyes. "Come and join me," he said gently.

She hesitated, her hands curling into the pleats of her skirt, the fabric whispering under her fingers. "What's wrong, Ria?"

"I — Uh. I just came to return your dagger." She stammered as she drew the silver blade from beneath her sash and offered it back, the metal gleaming pale in the dim afternoon light.

He examined her face, searching for some hidden truth. "Why? I gave you the blade so you could defend yourself."

"But in doing so, you gave up your defense," she tried to explain. Her voice trembled slightly, the words uncertain, like the quiver of candlelight. She was confused when he merely smiled.

"Hardly."

He held out his hand, and she stepped closer, her pulse thrumming as his warmth met hers. She let him guide her until she sat gingerly in his lap, the soft creak of the chair the only sound between them.

"That is a last resort weapon. If I need it, then I'm so far lost that all I would use it for is to take my own life."

Ria blinked in shock, her breath catching. "Would you — kill yourself?"

She had a hard time believing what she heard. The disbelief pulsed through their bond, raw and bright, and he felt it ripple through him.

"If I'm down to that dagger," he said quietly, "it means that I've gone through all my spells, my staff has been shattered, and there is no escape."

His eyes darkened with memory, but his tone was calm. "I'd rather die than be taken prisoner."

He drew her closer until she could feel the slow, steady beat of his heart against her own. "The fact that I'm giving up my last line of defense should tell you how much I love you."

It did. The truth of it filled her, spilling warmth through her chest until her soul sang for joy. She had finally found another man who loved her as deeply as Garion once had.

"It's a beautiful dagger, but not my style." She held onto the sheath, tracing its silver filigree with her fingertips. "Could we go find a dagger that would be mine alone?"

"Of course, we can, mo ghràidh," he whispered. "We can find you a suitable blade."

She fidgeted, her voice a soft rush of eagerness. "Can we do it now?"

Instead of answering, he gave her a playful push from his lap and rose to his feet.

The light from the window shifted, gilding his hair and the fine lines at the corners of his eyes. With a serene expression, he released her hip and took her hand, their fingers intertwining naturally.

Her smile said it all, and happiness radiated through the bond as they left the study together.

The corridor outside was cooler, scented faintly of polished wood and lavender oil. Their steps echoed softly off stone floors as they descended the stairs.

"You mentioned that you've never carried a knife before," Rhyslin commented, his tone thoughtful.

Ria nodded silently, the hem of her skirt brushing against the stair treads.

"May I ask why?"

"I stayed at home, behind the walls, surrounded by almost two hundred soldiers," she said, her cheeks coloring. "I never had a reason to carry one."

Rhyslin made a low, non-committal sound. "I can understand that. Why, now, do you want to carry a weapon?"

She paused mid-step, uncertain. "I no longer have two hundred soldiers," she began, then shook her head. "No, that's not why."

They stopped in the middle of the hall, where the light from the tall windows fell in long amber stripes across the floor. "I don't know. It didn't bother me until I was suddenly surrounded by all these strange men in our house." Her eyes lifted to his, filled with the memory of unease. "And then you surprised me this afternoon, and I realized that any man could do that, and I couldn't even hope to get away."

Rhyslin raised an eyebrow. "That isn't all, is it?"

Ria shook her head, her dark hair brushing her shoulders. "It hit me that I'm the only one who can't defend myself should something happen." She reached up and caressed his cheek. "I have two bond sisters and a daughter to stay alive for." She snorted softly. "Does it make sense?"

"It does," Rhyslin acknowledged. "You have a family that would miss you and one that you would blame yourself for if anything bad happened."

She smiled faintly, relieved that he understood.

The old draoidh did indeed understand. "You have the right to carry a weapon any time you want to, but remember that a dagger isn't an offensive weapon."

Ria blinked. "Then what is it?"

"It's a defensive weapon," Rhyslin explained. "The best use of a dagger, poniard, or stiletto is to surprise anyone who tried to kidnap you and make him release you so that you can run."

As they resumed their slow walk through the hall, the sound of their footsteps blended with the sigh of wind through the narrow windows.

Ria was so raptly paying attention that she barely noticed where they were going. "How does that work?"

He nodded, pleased by her curiosity. "A short-bladed knife is not what some men consider a dangerous weapon, but it doesn't take a long blade to cut the artery in the back of the leg, or rake a throat, jab an eye, or puncture a lung when you bury it between the ribs. You can get away and run for safety in that brief moment of surprise."

Ria ran her fingers through her hair, thinking. "I see." The faint scent of her perfume mingled with the air. "Can you teach me where to strike?"

"Of course," Rhyslin agreed. "I wouldn't give you a weapon if you didn't know how to use it."

When she stared at him, he chuckled. "I let you borrow that dagger so you'd feel safer around all these strange men." His shrug was easy, his tone untroubled. "I didn't see enough threat today to worry about it."

She drew a slow breath, steadying herself. "What's changed?"

"We'll be going to the council meeting in two days."

He stopped and gently turned her face toward his. The hall light caught the faint silver in his eyes.

"There will be substantially more than two hundred freeholders there. Some of them will have their soldiers with them. There's a greater chance that something could happen, and I want you to be prepared."

Ria's breath hitched. She hadn't expected so many. Though she had stood in grander courts before, something about this gathering filled her with quiet dread.

Rhyslin studied her face and noted each flicker of emotion, dread, awe, fear, resignation. "It'll be okay, mo ghràidh. I won't let anything happen to the four of you."

"The four?" Ria's brow furrowed. "You're not taking Rana, are you?"

When he merely gazed at her, she knew the answer. The weight of it pressed against her chest. "Yes, Maighstir," she murmured.

"I have to take you and Flur, and Rowena would kill me if I left her behind again," he said calmly. "As for Rana, this is part of her education. She needs to learn and understand how the council works." His eyes softened. "She may never have a Saor-Shelb, but knowing what the council does is important."

Ria lowered her eyes. "You're right, Maighstir. I was out of line."

"No, you weren't." His smile was weary but kind. "You are her mother and have a say in her life."

"Even if her destiny is already written?"

"Her destiny is scarcely written in stone," the old draoidh said gently. "Every day that she's here, that doom changes." His gaze turned distant. "Even Despoina can't see the end path."

Ria rested against him, her arms sliding around his waist, and felt the steady thrum of his heart through his robes. The scent of his skin—ash, parchment, a hint of lavender—settled her spirit. "When do we leave for the council?"

"In two days, more or less," he murmured, his breath stirring her hair. Then, more lightly, "Let's go find you a knife before we join the others in bed."

Ria nodded, falling into step beside Rhyslin as he led her toward the armory. The corridor they walked was quiet, lit by the warm amber glow of late afternoon sunlight filtering through the high windows. Dust motes danced in the shafts of light, lending the old stones a honeyed hue.

As they approached the heavy wooden door of the armory, the scent of oiled leather, steel, and ash greeted her like a breath from another world, sharp, utilitarian, and grounded.

Inside, the armory was cool and dim, the stone walls lined with racks of weapons that gleamed faintly under wrought-iron lanterns. Rows of swords, daggers, bows, and other instruments of war were carefully arranged in polished order. The faint metallic tang of steel mingled with the earthy smell of worn scabbards and cured hides. Rhyslin moved with practiced ease between the aisles, his fingers occasionally brushing over a hilt or pausing to glance at an inscription.

Ria followed, her eyes scanning the gleaming blades until one caught her attention, a thin-bladed stiletto with an elegant hilt and a subtle wave to its pattern.

She plucked it from its mount and held it out with a proud smile, her voice light with satisfaction. She lifted the hem of her skirt just enough, revealing a pale expanse of thigh, and handed the sheath to Rhyslin.

"You do realize that I'm going to have to slit my skirt pocket so that I can get to it without flashing everyone." She playfully groused as she teased him.

Rhyslin's eyes sparkled with mischief as he knelt and strapped the leather sheath to her right thigh, the buckle snug but comfortable against her skin.

"Why ever would you want to do that?" he said, "Seeing you lift your skirt would send a rational man packing, then seeing the blade would drive him to panic.”

Suddenly feeling so much better,Ria laughed softly, the sound echoing like wind chimes off the stone.

“Hush, only you get to see under my skirt.”

“Maybe I should keep you at home when I attend the council meeting,” Rhyslin stated as he scratched his chin, a playful edge in his voice.

“Oh no, you don’t,” she complained. “You can’t tell me I’m going and then change your mind.” She stepped closer to him, the leather of her boots whispering against the stone floor, and raised her head to kiss him. “I lost so much time with Garion when he traveled. I won’t make the same mistake again.”

When she pulled away and took a breath, Rhyslin inhaled, tasting the sweet trace of her presence on the air, like rose petals warmed by sunlight.

“I will always be glad to have you travel with me. Nor will I ever stop you.”

The former Banrig gave him a dazzling smile, brushing her fingers through her hair as she admired the way the stiletto hugged her thigh.

"It's so light, I almost forgot it was there," she said, referring to the stiletto. "I wish there were a way I could wear it around my neck or hide it in my hair," she mused as she took Rhyslin's hand and held it.

"There may be a way," he said as they left the armory and closed the heavy door behind them.

The latch clicked shut, muffling the metallic hush within. "I'll have to search my library and see what I can find."

Ria giggled softly, her voice as light as the rustle of silk in the empty hall. "Don't concern yourself too much with it," she said happily. "For now, it is fine."

"If you are sure," he commented, his eyes never leaving hers.

"I am, mo ghràidh as truime," she whispered. "As always, you set my mind at ease." Her sincerity shimmered through the bond, warm and unguarded. "I have had this tendency to worry about things of no consequence." She gazed at him, a wistful smile brushing her lips, thinking about how one day, she would sing for him.

✦ ✦ ✦

The first rays of dawn spilled across the horizon, gilding the peaks beyond the valley and washing Rhyslin's balcony in soft gold. He stood there in quiet meditation, the crisp morning air brushing against his skin as he breathed in the scent of dew and woodsmoke rising from the lower halls.

The draoidh's silver hair stirred faintly in the breeze, catching the sun as he listened to the stillness, the faint birdsong from the eaves, the distant clatter of servants stirring below, the quiet hum of power within the stones of the manor.

Behind him, his council garments lay neatly folded on a carved oaken chair. Kenna had taken it upon herself to prepare them, and she'd done well, if one didn't count the faint scent of singed silk clinging to his white shirt.

The black cotton pants had fared better, the dark fabric hiding any evidence of heat. Rhyslin had smiled at her earnest effort, rewarding the cat girl with gentle scritches behind her ears before sending her on her way.

Now, he waited, patient as the dawn, for the four women of his household to join him.

The first to emerge was Rana. She stepped out into the sunlight with the fresh, open energy of youth, dressed in a teal blouse and skirt, her black half-boots gleaming. Her hazel eyes sparkled as she tilted her face toward the rising sun, light catching in her carefully brushed hair until it shimmered like fine bronze thread.

"Good morrow, Maighstir Rhyslin. I can carry my sword, right?"

When he nodded, she fastened her sword belt around her hips with deliberate care, the leather creaking softly. "Good." She walked over and hugged him, the scent of lavender clinging faintly to her. "I would have left it behind if you had asked me to."

"Good morrow, Rhyslin," Rowena offered as she stepped outside and faced the sun. Her dark cloak rippled faintly in the morning wind, contrasting sharply with the pale sky.

Beneath it, the glint of silver embroidery along her blouse caught his eye, a quiet display of elegance hidden beneath shadow.

"Do you have your poniard?" he inquired, admiring her composure.

She nodded, her hand brushing the hidden hilt beneath her skirt. "Good," he murmured, satisfied.

A sudden laugh, bright and golden, heralded Flur's arrival. A wave of sunlight followed her into the open air, gleaming across her braid as she threw her arms around Rhyslin in a hug that left him breathless.

"Good morning, Maighstir mo gràidh," she whispered in his ear.

She stepped back and twirled in the sunlight, her sky-blue blouse catching the light like silk water. The darker blue skirt flared with her spin, folding gracefully around her knees as she came to a stop.

Her braid, long and golden, swung like spun sunlight down her back.

"I've got mine," she said with a proud smile, resting her hand over her thigh where the hilt of her poniard was hidden beneath the folds of her skirt. "What do you think?"

Rhyslin whistled softly under his breath. "They won't know what hit them."

Her grin deepened, cheeks flushed with delight.

All that remained was Ria. Rhyslin waited, anticipation building like a held breath. Then she appeared at the top of the stairs, framed by the sun streaming through the window behind her, and for a moment, he forgot to breathe.

To say she looked radiant was like saying the sun shone. Her raven-dark hair had been woven into an intricate braid that circled her head like a crown, while the rest fell in soft waves down her back.

Her green silk dress shimmered with every movement, silver beads catching the light like morning dew on leaves. On her feet, simple sandals whispered against the polished floor.

Unlike the others, Ria wore her stiletto at her waist, openly, confidently, a quiet statement of her resolve.

She tasted his prana, savoring his wordless admiration through their bond. A slow, dazzling smile bloomed across her lips as she moved to his side.

"Do you like it?"

"Oh yes," Rhyslin said with a half-bow. "You will be the talk of the council."

Ria preened, pleased by his reaction, then glanced toward the stairs. "Do you suppose Allanagh and Mayana are ready?"

Rhyslin shrugged lightly. "They should be. I can hear Sloan and Silas talking downstairs."

He waited a heartbeat, listening to the distant murmur of male voices echoing up the stairwell. "Let's head downstairs and see if everyone else is ready."

Rana, ever curious, was the first to follow him. "Maighstir, how many are going with us?"

Rhyslin paused, his staff tapping softly against the floor. "Sloan, Allanah, four soldiers. Silas, Mayana, four soldiers. Us and five soldiers. Marcus, Natolii, and four guards. Rembran, Ixa, and Andros. All told, thirty-one people."

Rana blinked. "That's a lot of blood," she marveled. "Who are we sacrificing?" she teased.

"Nobody," Rhyslin replied, deadpan. "We will have to use the transport chamber."

"What's a transport chamber?" Flur asked, tilting her head as she fell into step behind him.

The draoidh half-turned, his cloak brushing the stairs. "It's how we will travel twelve leagues to the council hall," he explained, his fingers drumming absently against the ebony wood of his staff. "When the others are ready, we'll leave the chamber."

"Is it like Mathair's gateway?" Ria asked, remembering the luminous silver archway she had once passed through.

Rhyslin's expression softened with thought. "It's similar, but we don't have access to her levels of draoidheachd. We have to..." He shook his head faintly. "It's easier to show you."

They descended the stairway in companionable silence, the soft fall of boots and the faint rustle of skirts filling the hall.

The foyer below was alive with quiet activity, guards checking weapons, servants adjusting cloaks, the faint crackle of the hearth fire warming the air.

Moments later, the others joined them. Makar, Sloan, and Silas entered first, each man's attire a reflection of his temperament and homeland. Makar's reddish-gold shirt and earth-toned cloak seemed to glow in the firelight. Sloan's black-on-black attire absorbed the brightness, giving him the air of a shadow given form, while Silas's gray cloak and brown shirt made him look carved from the forest itself.

Then came Allanagh and Mayana, and for a moment, the foyer seemed to still.

If the men were dressed for war, the women were dressed for reign. Allanagh's forest-green gown shimmered with golden jewels that caught the firelight like stars.

Her silver hair, swept into a spiral crown, revealed delicate ears and the quiet confidence of a queen who had once commanded nations. At her side, her dagger glimmered proudly, worn where all could see.

Mayana, by contrast, was dawn to Allanagh's forest dusk. Her sky-blue dress shimmered with threads of red and silver that echoed her hair, her green eyes bright with calm amusement as she lingered near Silas. If she carried a weapon, it was hidden well.

"Eh, Rhyslin." Makar's voice rumbled warmly as he approached. "There are going to be an awful lot of us.

Will you be able to transport us to your council meeting?"

"I will," Rhyslin admitted, then turned to the two queens with a wry smile. "You both look lovely. If the council isn't careful, they'll give whatever you want and won't know why."

Mayana blushed faintly, lowering her gaze. "Thank you, ar dìonadair," she murmured. "We weren't sure how to dress." Allanagh nodded beside her, regal yet faintly amused.

"You both look ravishing." Rhyslin smiled, the warmth in his tone softening the formality of his words. "I am surrounded by beauty that would make other men green with envy." He turned his gaze toward the three Hin I-Balanath leaders. "If you don't take offense, I'll give you the same warning I gave my bannaichean."

When the men nodded, he continued, his voice steady and low. "There will be over two hundred free-holders in attendance, along with whatever soldiers they've hired to protect them. If you have weapons, make sure you are carrying them. If you are challenged, it's up to you to accept."

He paused. "Nobody will think any less of you should you refuse until the treaties are signed. Then you'll be expected to defend yourself and your own."

"As it should be," Sloan muttered, his tone edged with iron.

"Hear, hear," Makar echoed, crossing his arms. "A true man never retreats from honorable combat."

Silas, ever measured, looked toward Rhyslin. "Is this all of us? Are we still waiting on someone?"

"We are waiting on Marcus, Natolie, Rembran, Ixa, and Andros. They should be waiting near the transport chamber."

"Ah," Makar rumbled, nodding once. "Shall we get going then?"

The group began to move, the air alive with the rustle of fabric and the faint jingle of metal.

Outside, the sun had climbed fully above the horizon, flooding the courtyard with light, and far below, the hidden chamber pulsed faintly with restrained magic, waiting for its travelers.

Chapter Nine

The Summons to the Council

Rhyslin nodded, leading the way out of the foyer. The heavy doors of the Mansion closed behind them with a muted thud, muffling the echoing corridors within. Outside, the air was cool and crisp, touched with the faint sweetness of wet stone and cedar from the gardens. Moonlight filtered through the mist clinging to the grounds, and the gravel path beneath their boots gave a soft, steady crunch as they moved.

He turned left, guiding his unlikely company along a winding path that spiraled toward the Mansion's flank, where a glass-enclosed structure shimmered faintly in the night. The building's panes caught the lanternlight like captured starlight, each reflection trembling slightly in the faint wind.

As they approached, five silhouettes stood waiting in the dim glow beyond.

"It took you long enough," Marcus quipped as he stepped out of the shadows.

"*Manducare stercore et mori,*" Rhyslin retorted dryly, his tone as sharp as the gleam of moonlight on his staff. His gaze flicked over Marcus and Natolie, taking in the familiar details with a faint glint of affection he didn't voice. Marcus was dressed in what could only be called a dress uniform: a navy shirt pressed to perfection, dark trousers tucked into polished black boots, and his color-shifting cloak that rippled like oil on water when he moved.

Natolie, by contrast, was all radiance and fire. Her long red sheath dress caught the low light, its lace trim glimmering faintly around the bust.

Her hair, flame-red and abundant, spilled down her back, the ends brushing the curve of her waist like living silk. When she smiled, the warmth of it seemed to cut through the chill lingering on the air.

The Sealgair Aisling walked forward and embraced the draoidh. Her perfume was faint but earthy, jasmine and woodsmoke. "It's good to see you again, Rhyslin." Her hug was given and withdrawn with practiced grace, and she turned her attention to Rana. "Good morrow, Rana. I don't know how you did it, but you impressed Angelica."

The spellblade inclined her head. "Good morrow, Mistress Natolie." She smiled broadly. "I don't know how I could have done that. She surprised me when we first met."

"Nevertheless," Natolie commented, "Angelica doesn't talk about other people but hasn't stopped talking about you, especially how you almost beat Marcus in your first duel."

"I would have won were it not for that vine," Rana smirked.

The ranger's laughter came easily, low and warm. "The lightning strikes were very effective. Luckily, the tree grounded most of them." He gestured toward the building, whose glass walls reflected the light of the Mansion behind them. "After we get through with this council meeting and get back, your next lesson will be archery."

Rana grinned. "That would be wonderful."

Marcus dismissed her with a nod, the mirth in his eyes fading to focus as he addressed Rhyslin. "Rembran, Ixa, and Andros are waiting inside."

"Good," the draoidh replied, exhaling through his nose. "The sooner we get there, the sooner we can get it over with."

The ranger studied him for a moment, eyes narrowing slightly as the wind tugged at his cloak. "Do you think you'll have enough energy to transport all of us to Aus Town?"

Rhyslin blew out a slow breath that misted faintly in the cool air. "I should. At the very least, I'll be able to transport everyone there. As for getting back, we'll see."

"Okay, how do you want to do this?" Marcus asked, following Rhyslin into the glass building.

Inside, the air was cooler still, carrying the faint metallic tang of old magic. The light from outside refracted through the panes, scattering faint prisms across the tiled floor.

A distant hum, like the echo of a harp string, resonated through the walls, the sound of latent draoidheachd waiting to be stirred.

Rhyslin paused inside the doorway, his senses brushing the auras of those waiting within. "Rembran, Ixa, Andros," he greeted quietly. His voice seemed to settle into the chamber, absorbed by the still air. He reached toward a glass orb fastened to the wall and whispered, "*Biodh solas ann.*"

Light blossomed from the orb, swelling gently until it filled the room with a steady glow. The shadows retreated, revealing the chamber in its full, deliberate beauty. The lower half of the walls was built of red brick, warm and earthen; above that, the blue stone gleamed faintly, like sky trapped in stone. The ceiling swirled with white and grey paint, giving the illusion of shifting clouds caught in perpetual motion.

Small, rounded windows punctuated the walls every few feet, each painted with symbols of the gods that shimmered faintly under the new light.

Rembran and his companions slunk along the walls, their boots whispering against the floor as they took up quiet positions. Marcus and Natolie flanked the door like twin sentinels, one shadow, one flame.

As the first party filtered in, Marcus asked, "In what order would you like us to go?"

Rhyslin considered, the glow from the orb catching the pale edges of his eyes as he crossed to the panel at the back.

"I think it might be better for you and Natolie to lead the way, then Silas, Mayana, and their four soldiers. Next in sequence will be Sloan, Allanagh, and their four soldiers. After that, Makar and his four soldiers.

Then myself, my bhanna, and Rana." He nodded to himself, satisfied with the order.

"What about us?" Rembran inquired from the far corner, his voice a rough murmur that barely carried.

"You can travel with Marcus and Natolie." Rhyslin's tone was clipped but not unkind. He turned as the rest took their places along the walls. "We won't teleport directly into the Council chamber for obvious reasons. The receiving hall is on the grounds, and roughly ten *mionaidean*'s walk from the hall." His gaze swept the assembly. "You can either wait for me or follow Marcus to the Council Hall."

Sloan's eyes darted to the floor, where the faint shimmer of carved sigils could be seen, five of them along the golden circle's edge and one set in its center.

"We travel in groups of six, then?" he asked, recognizing the pattern.

"Yes," Rhyslin admitted. "Marcus will go first, then Silas and his five, then you, then Makar, and I will go last."

"Why should you go last?" The dark-skinned Hin I-Balanath General's voice carried a low challenge, softened only by the deep respect threading beneath it.

"Somebody has to control the teleport. Rembran has never used this device, and the only other person that I would have trusted, betrayed the Saorsa." Rhyslin's voice was low, the words carrying the faint tremor of a wound not yet closed.

The sound of it seemed to linger in the chamber like the fading toll of a bell. The betrayal still cut too deeply; even the air around him felt heavier for it.

He had placed a lot of trust in Meron, too much, perhaps, and now that trust hung like an echo in the spaces between breaths.

"How does this work?" Silas inquired as he led Mayanna and his soldiers to stand along the wall behind the console. Their boots clicked against the smooth stone, each sound swallowed quickly by the hush of expectation.

"In theory, it's just like A' Mathair's gateway, but not as fancy. One moment, you'll be here, the next there."

A faint hum seemed to rise from the floor, the sound of contained energy waiting to be given purpose.

The golden inlay of the teleport circle shimmered softly, as if it had been waiting for his touch.

Ever curious, Rana slipped away from the group and examined the console.

The crystal panels reflected her face in a thousand soft distortions, her eyes wide with wonder. "You said we don't need to sacrifice of ourselves, right?"

"Correct," Rhyslin nodded again. "The chamber collects the ambient draoidheachd and uses it to transport us."

She tilted her head, studying the intricate lattice of sigils that pulsed faintly beneath the glass. The faint scent of ozone and warm stone filled the room.

"May I watch you work?" the spellblade asked. "I won't get in your way or touch anything."

"Of course, you may." Rhyslin moved to stand behind the console, the folds of his cloak whispering over the floor. "Do you mind holding my staff?"

He handed the awestruck spellblade his ebonwood staff.

As her fingers closed around the polished shaft, it hummed softly, resonating with her presence. A faint smile crossed her lips as it sang to her, a deep, mellow tone like the voice of the wind through a cavern.

"Marcus."

"On it," the ranger commented. His voice broke the reverent stillness as he stepped forward. "Come on, Rembran."

He strode into the golden circle and took his customary spot at its center. His boots gave a low creak as he shifted his stance, the color-shifting cloak at his shoulders gleaming faintly under the light. "Natolie, Rembran, Ixa, Andros—outer edge," he instructed, and they moved in near-perfect unison to their places around the rim of the circle. The air in the room seemed to tighten with expectation.

When Marcus was satisfied that everyone was in position, he turned toward Rhyslin and gave the signal, one hand curled into a fist, the other flat across its top.

The draoidh inclined his head slightly, his expression serene but intent. He looked down, and his fingers began to move. They danced across the console with deft precision, tapping the gems set into its surface in a sequence too fast to follow.

Each touch awoke a faint glow: amethyst, topaz, sapphire, and emerald flaring in rhythmic succession. With his right hand, he traced the sigils in sequence; with his left, his finger drew a complex shape upon the clear crystal panel, leaving behind trails of pale light that faded as quickly as breath.

As the onlookers watched, the room itself seemed to respond.

The windows brightened, the colored panes alive with divine symbols that shimmered like living things. The red and blue bricks of the chamber walls caught the growing light, reflecting it in waves that seemed to pulse with the rhythm of his movements.

The air thickened with the scent of charged energy, metallic, dry, and faintly sweet, as draoidheachd gathered from within the chamber and beyond it, drawn by invisible threads into the waiting circle.

Rhyslin closed his eyes. His breathing slowed, and the energy in the air bent toward him like grass before the wind. The faint vibrations of magic thrummed underfoot, steady as a heartbeat. Shadows trembled on the walls as he reached through them, feeling for the thread that would open the right path.

His mind stretched across leagues, searching the weave between worlds until the resonance snapped into alignment.

An emerald set in the console's top corner flashed twice. Rhyslin exhaled softly, the release of tension almost imperceptible.

Then Marc's voice came through, muffled but clear, carried along the same pulse of magic. "We made it, Rhyslin. Give us just a few seconds to get the lights functioning."

From the other end came the faint clatter of metal scraping stone, followed by a brief string of soft curses. A moment later: "Thank you, Nat."

Rhyslin's lips twitched. He could almost picture it, Marcus colliding with a wall in the dark, Natolie catching him with a single, unamused glance. The thought warmed him more than he'd expected.

Marcus coughed over the link, his voice steady once again. "We are ready to receive the next group."

The emerald gem pulsed once more in response, casting ripples of green light across Rhyslin's face. The chamber, now still and waiting, seemed to hold its breath for the next act.

Rhyslin opened his eyes only when the other console sent a faint pulse through the air, a shimmer that rippled along the surface of the crystal like a heartbeat felt through glass. It was the subtle signal that Natolie had taken control on the far end. The tension in his shoulders eased slightly. Drawing in a long breath scented with stone dust and residual ozone, he called out, "Silas, take your group and get ready."

Without a word, the hin I-Balanath moved with quiet purpose, his boots thudding softly against the polished floor.

His soldiers fell in behind him, their armor giving off muted clinks as they arranged themselves. The way he positioned his men, forming a protective ring with Mayanna at the center, spoke volumes about where his loyalties lay.

Rhyslin watched them with steady focus, his fingers lightly brushing the console's edge. When Silas echoed Marcus's earlier signal, Rhyslin's hands began to move. The console stirred to life once more, the sigils across its face burning in a sequence of soft light, white, then green, then gold. The air thickened, humming as though it were alive.

A moment later, the draoidheachd gathered like a rising tide, threading through the circle before releasing with a sound like a sigh. The shimmer of magic folded inward, and the six figures dissolved in a cascade of pale light. The circle fell dark again, leaving behind the faint scent of rain and static.

Rhyslin waited, his breath caught in his throat until the answering tug rippled back through the console, confirmation of safe arrival.

Only then did he exhale and murmur a silent prayer of thanks to the gods that Natolie was overseeing the receiving hall. Her steadiness was a balm to the edges of his worry.

He gestured toward Sloan next, who wordlessly motioned his men and Allanagh forward. The general's eyes swept the room, calm and deliberate. The gold sigils on his vambraces flickered faintly in the light. He didn't use Marcus's gesture; instead, he simply met Rhyslin's gaze and nodded once.

The draoidh touched the crystal with two fingers. There was a brief, resonant hum, deep as a drumbeat, and Sloan's group vanished in a spiral of blue light that left motes drifting like fireflies in the air.

The energy in the room grew warmer now, the air vibrating faintly with each new sending.

Sweat gathered along Rhyslin's temple despite the chill stone underfoot. In quick succession, Makar and his soldiers took their turn, the pulse of magic stronger now, faster, echoing off the curved glass walls like the breath of the gods themselves.

When the chamber fell quiet again, only Rhyslin's own group remained. The flickering glow from the console painted shifting shadows across their faces, Rana's bright and expectant, the bhanna's calm and resolute.

"Rana, do me a favor and step into the center," Rhyslin requested.

Her brow furrowed in surprise, but she complied, moving gracefully across the circle. The faint hum of draoidheachd seemed to follow her steps.

"I need your spot. It's closest to the console."

Rana nodded, the movement lit by the emerald reflections that chased each other across her armor. She took her place in the center, standing perfectly still, her hand resting lightly on the ebonwood staff she still carried.

Rhyslin tapped the glowing emerald on the console. Its surface shimmered like the surface of a deep pool.

"Nat, can you give me a ten count, then bring us across?"

"Of course, Maighstir Darkblade," the sealgair aisling's voice replied through the link, calm, precise, and warm with familiarity.

Rhyslin stepped out from behind the console, the quiet thud of his boots echoing in the wide chamber.

The magic in the air grew thicker, pressing against his skin like invisible wind. He moved to his place in the circle and began counting down in his mind.

Ten... nine... eight... the low hum deepened. The sigils flared.

Three... two... one—

The world folded.

For a heartbeat, there was only light and movement, a rushing pressure that filled his lungs and ears. The air around him warped, folding space into itself, and the smell of lightning filled his senses. Then the pressure broke, and solid ground returned beneath his boots.

As the teleport spell released him, Rhyslin stumbled, his knees buckling slightly under the sudden shift.

He reached instinctively for his staff, only to remember it wasn't there. The moment of imbalance steadied when he saw Rana already holding it out to him, her expression half concern, half pride.

"Thank you," he whispered, taking the staff and grounding himself again. The wood's familiar hum steadied the ringing in his ears. He gave a brief look around, ensuring his bhanna were uninjured, their faces illuminated by the soft light of the receiving hall.

The air here was cooler, thinner, touched by the faint scent of old incense and stone dust. A soft green luminescence came from runes carved into the walls, casting long shadows that flickered as the portal energy faded.

Rhyslin walked over to Natolie, whose hands were still resting lightly on the receiver console. He raised his right hand. "Thank you for working this end."

The red-haired sealgair aisling smiled, the light catching on her copper hair like living fire. She raised her right hand and pressed it to his.

"It was my honor, Maighstir." Her touch was firm, respectful, an unspoken exchange between equals.

Her gaze drifted toward Marcus, who was rubbing his right shoulder with a grimace.

Rhyslin followed her eyes and couldn't resist the jab. "I can't take you anywhere that you don't try to bring down the walls."

Marcus grunted, rolling his shoulder. "You know me; walls are my enemy." His chuckle bounced faintly off the chamber walls. "I forgot how dark it was in here. Why didn't you ever put windows in this one?"

Rhyslin shrugged, his voice echoing softly. "We didn't have any here, and it's so rarely used that I didn't think it was necessary."

Natolie stepped to Marcus's side, her crimson silhouette bright against the pale stone. "It might be worth looking into, sir. I just barely had enough draoidheachd to activate it and keep it functional. If it hadn't been drawing from the sending terminal—" She shrugged lightly, her tone matter-of-fact despite the lingering fatigue in her eyes.

"You might be right, Nat. I'll look into it," Rhyslin replied. "If other council members want to use it, they'd need mages, and very few have the reserves."

The sealgair aisling dipped her head at the praise. She laid a gentle hand on Marcus's shoulder, whispering a few quiet words beneath her breath. A faint pulse of gold light passed from her palm, and the ranger's grimace eased into a grateful smile.

The group stood for a few moments in the soft hum of residual magic, the faint glow from the console fading to a steady, heartbeat rhythm. Outside the tall stone doors, distant footsteps and muted voices hinted at the life of the Council Hall beyond.

Rhyslin adjusted his cloak and gestured toward the door. The movement caught the emerald gleam of his staff. "Let's go," he murmured.

Rembran, Ixa, and Andros moved first, their forms shifting into motion like well-trained shadows. One by one, the others followed, their footfalls echoing softly through the corridor as they made their way toward the Council Hall, and whatever awaited them within.

Chapter Ten

The Challenge in the Council Hall

The curved path from the receiving hall unfurled before them like a ribbon of pale stone edged in moss. Sunlight streamed through the open colonnade, gilding the air with warmth and the faint scent of lilac and pine resin. The hum of insects and the whisper of leaves filled the silences between their footsteps.

As they walked, the group passed through two small flower gardens. Each garden was a living mosaic, beds of violets and lilies surrounded by ferns that swayed as though stirred by an unseen breath. In the heart of each stood a tree older than the buildings around it, its roots veined through soil and marble alike.

Within each tree's hollow, the soft shimmer of spirit-light betrayed the presence of a dryad. The caretakers emerged as they passed, their translucent forms wreathed in green and gold. Laughter like windchimes filled the air as they rushed to Rhyslin, arms open, asking for hugs with childlike delight.

After passing through both gardens and bidding the dryads farewell, Makar slowed and then stopped. His boots crunched softly over the gravel path as he gestured toward the nearest garden. "Is this a recurring motif?" His weathered hand encompassed the blooms, the trees, the faint motes of light dancing between branches.

Rhyslin paused beside him and smiled faintly. "It is." He looked around, letting his gaze linger on the dappling of sunlight across the petals. "Would you rather everything be stone and mortar?"

The hin I-Balanath general considered this, his gaze traveling from the green canopy above to the bright flowers near his feet. "Of course not," he admitted after a moment. "It's just not what I expected." His eyes followed a dryad as she knelt, her hands buried in the soil at the base of her tree. "I don't know what I expected." A furrow formed between his brows, and a faint, almost embarrassed flush rose along his dark cheeks. "I just imagined it would be more militaristic."

Marcus turned at that, the light from his shifting cloak scattering faint color across the path. "Every male citizen is armed, and most are part of the military," he said, "but we rarely set foot outside of our own country."

His tone carried the weight of long experience, though it softened when Rhyslin shook his head.

"We've only had two contracts that are outside the country," Marcus continued, holding up a finger. "We have a contingent in the old Imperial March, mainly because the current Marquise hired us to protect his trade routes. The others work for Rhyslin, and they go where he wants to go. The last journey was to the far side of the Bazan Confederacy, where we stopped an attack on a certain Hin I-Balanath fort."

Makar's eyes shifted instinctively toward Allanagh. She blushed, her freckles darkening, and quickly looked away, pretending to study the cobblestones.

"Ah, I see," Makar replied, a faint smile tugging at the corner of his mouth. "Do all of your cities have groves and gardens?" His voice carried genuine curiosity now, warmed by awe.

The gentle air, rich with fragrance and the low music of bees, seemed to soften even the veteran's edges.

"Yes, they do," Rhyslin commented. "And the Dryads all pushed for it. It helps balance nature with civilization, which was always my goal when I helped plan village layouts." He glanced up the hill to where the Council Hall's marble gleamed through the trees. The tall monolith beside it cast a long, clear shadow across the grass, marking the hour like the finger of the gods. By his estimate, they had only a few minutes before the council convened.

They resumed walking, their footsteps echoing softly on the curved path. Two more gardens awaited them, each alive with birdsong and the scent of wet earth.

In the third, a small fountain caught the sun, sending shards of light across the leaves like scattered gems.

"Admit it, old friend," Makar grumbled as they reached the final garden. "You made us take this circuitous route just to show off the gardens." His words were playful, but the way his fingers brushed the trunk of a tree betrayed something gentler. Though he tried to sound piqued, he couldn't hide the quiet reverence on his face.

He wanted to linger there, to breathe in the green calm that the Saorsa had built, but memory caught him off guard. The laughter in the leaves turned into the rustle of desert wind. The scent of loam became the dry sting of sand. His face fell as he remembered the oasis, the home he and his people would soon abandon.

For a moment, his face darkened as memory overtook him.

Rhyslin noticed the look and slowed. "That wasn't my intent, Makar," he said quietly. "I thought you'd like to see what we learned from your people, in this case, Allanagh's faction." His tone carried the weight of shared history.

The old general's shoulders eased, his expression softening as he met Rhyslin's eyes. "Thank you, my friend." He sighed, his voice low but resolute. "These talks can't fail. I won't let them."

The words hung between them, solemn as an oath.

They turned the final bend, and the Council Hall came into view, a marvel of artistry and power. The three-tiered structure rose from the hillside like a mountain carved into symmetry. Its marble façade shimmered in hues of grey, white, and black, veined through with streaks of blue that caught the morning light.

The stained-glass windows blazed with color, amber, crimson, and sea-green, echoing those Rhyslin had crafted for the transport chamber at Am Flur Manse. The bronze-hued doors were bound with silvered steel bolts, framed by open marble columns that reached skyward like the fingers of giants.

The visitors halted, struck silent by the grandeur. For the Hin I-Balanath, whose cities were of sandstone and sun, this mingling of stone and artistry felt near divine.

Rhyslin gave them a few moments to take it in before speaking. His voice was quiet but carried easily across the marble steps. "Remember, everyone is armed and will react as such. Try not to start anything, but don't let anyone take advantage of you."

The soldiers nodded, disciplined even in wonder. If Makar, Sloan, or Silas felt any unease, they didn't show it.

The air between them was tense but respectful, the kind that precedes diplomacy or battle.

Ria looked at the doors and closed her eyes, lips moving in silent prayer for peace. Flur stood beside her, hand resting lightly on the hilt of her weapon, a small grin playing across her mouth, ready, confident, almost eager.

But Rowena lingered behind them, her dark hair stirring in the faint breeze. Her eyes shimmered with worry, and the faint shimmer of foresight clouded them.

"Is something amiss?" Rhyslin inquired as he felt her unease through the bond.

Rowena's hair caught the sunlight as she shook her head. "It's frustrating not being able to see the future when I'm around you."

The draoidh arched a brow, his tone teasing as he started up the stairs. "Exciting, right?"

The seeress blinked, then groaned softly. "Please, don't do that. Exciting for you often turns into facing undead dragons."

His only answer was a wicked grin. The doors loomed above him, their bronze sheen rippling with reflected light as he reached to push them open.

The doors opened, and sound crashed over them like surf. Voices layered upon voices, arguments, laughter, the scrape of boots on marble, until the vast chamber seemed to breathe noise. Rana flinched and clapped her hands to her ears.

The interior stretched before them in disciplined geometry. Black and white marble gleamed beneath the high, vaulted ceiling, the pattern laid in twelve precise rows of twelve squares.

The alternation of light and dark created the illusion of motion, a living *tàileasg* board vast enough to hold a nation's fate. Each square cradled a single chair, one hundred and forty-four in total, their polished backs catching the glow from chandeliers suspended like frozen constellations.

The air smelled faintly of oil, parchment, and incense from the morning rites. It was cool here, the kind of cool that turned sound crisp and made every step echo with authority.

Along both sides of the hall, benches ran the length of the chamber. To the right sat the guests' section, empty save for a few dignitaries murmuring behind folded hands. To the left, the remaining freeholders, their eyes already fixed on the newcomers.

At the far end, a dais rose three steps above the marble floor.

Ten high-backed chairs of older design stood there, carved from ancient oak and bound with silver inlay.

The faint wear on their arms and cushions spoke of age and lineage, these were the seats of the First Freeholders, founders of the Saorsa. Their silent authority pressed down like a weight.

Rhyslin guided his companions forward, his boots whispering across the marble. He tapped Sloan on the shoulder and gestured toward the visitor benches. The Hin I-Balanath delegation moved with quiet discipline, their armor murmuring as they crossed the chessboard floor.

Rhyslin watched in faint amusement as they navigated between the alternating squares, dark, light, dark, careful not to mar the precision of the pattern. He turned toward his own chair at the head of the board.

That was when he heard the curse.

"Get out of my way, *thu 'n cù ban gòrach ann an teas.*[4]"

The words cracked through the air like a whip. Rhyslin spun just as a muscular man in a black dress uniform extended an arm in a brutal shove. Ria stumbled forward and fell hard, the sound of her knees striking marble cutting through the noise of the hall. Her dark hair spilled around her shoulders in a curtain of shame.

The man, a captain, by his silver epaulets and bearing, sneered down at her. His voice carried, dripping contempt.

---

[4] You stupid bitch in heat.

"I swear, you give *gnèithean creiche*[5] clothes and they think they are royalty."

He drew his leg back, ready to kick her where she knelt.

Before Rhyslin could move, motion like lightning flashed at the corner of his vision. A cascade of golden hair, a hiss of steel. Flur was already there. Her poniard gleamed in the cold light as she seized the captain by his beard and yanked him downward until his throat met the blade's fine edge.

The crowd gasped, a sudden collective intake of breath, and then silence fell so complete that even the chandeliers seemed to stop swaying.

Rhyslin froze where he stood. His usually serene *bhanna* was transformed, her beauty sharpened, her warmth gone. Her voice, when it came, was low and dangerous, like honey poured over a blade.

"You have insulted my *maighstir*, sister, and house."

The captain stiffened. His hands rose slowly in surrender, fingers trembling.

---

[5] You stupid bitch in heat.

The scent of his fear mingled with oil and metal. "Who are you? Who is your *maighstir*?"

Flur's grip did not waver. The muscles in her arm flexed as the edge pressed closer against the vulnerable skin of his neck. If he broke her hold, she would still cut him.

Her voice was a thing of ice and ceremony. "I am Flur Droigheann, *boireannach a' chiad cheangal*[6] and *Bana-mhaighstir nan Cridhe am Mansa flùr*[7] My *Maighstir* is Rhyslin Darkblade."

Each title landed with ritual weight. The captain's color drained with every word.

But Flur was not finished. With a fierce tug, she forced his head down until his eyes met Ria's, the woman he had struck.

"She is Ilyriatri Oran Roinag, *dàrna boireannach ceangailte*[8] and *Bana-mhaighstir an sporan am Mansa flùr*[9]. Her *Maighstir* is Rhyslin Darkblade."

---

[6] First Bond Woman

[7] .Mistress of Hearts at the House of Flowers.

[8] second bonded woman

[9] Mistress of the Purse at the House of Flowers

The captain's breath came shallow, his eyes darting toward the draoidh standing at the center of the hall. Rhyslin's gaze was cold enough to still the man's pulse.

Flur's poniard shifted again, its tip tracing the air until it pointed toward the dark-haired seeress watching from nearby. "She is Rowena, the Seeress of Despoina, *treas boireannach ceangailte am Mansa flùr*[10] Her *Maighstir* is Rhyslin Darkblade."

By now, sweat poured down the captain's face, beading along his temple and sliding down into his beard.

"By the gods, woman. I apologize for — " he stammered.

Flur's eyes narrowed. The sweetness in her voice returned, but it was the sweetness of venom. "I'm not the one you threw to the floor and threatened to kick." Her tone thickened with contempt. "She's the one you should apologize to," she loosened her grip slightly, "if you have honor, that is."

---

[10] third bonded woman at the House of Flowers.

The poniard's gleam lingered a moment longer at his throat, a single thread of silver light, before she drew it back. The captain's breath came ragged, the shame of his own cowardice louder than the hall's returning murmurs.

Ria still knelt on the cold marble, strands of hair trembling where they touched the floor. The vast chamber seemed to hold its breath, watching what kind of man he would prove to be.

The captain gulped again, his throat working visibly beneath the blade. The sharp scent of sweat and fear filled the air between them. His voice trembled when he whispered, "If I may?" a flick of his eyes gesturing toward the keen edge of Flur's poniard resting lightly over his carotid.

The golden-haired *bhanna* held his gaze, her blue eyes bright and cold as tempered steel. For a moment, the world seemed to shrink to the space between them, his pulse hammering beneath the knife, her steady breath calm as a priestess at vigil. Then, with a flutter of lashes that felt almost cruel, she lowered the blade and let the point fall away.

The captain exhaled sharply, wiping the sheen of sweat from his brow with a trembling hand. The sound of his boots echoed faintly on the marble as he took two cautious steps toward Ria.

He extended his hand, his voice hoarse but steady. "I beg your forgiveness, Lady Ilyriatri."

The hall had fallen silent, even the banners high above seemed to hold their breath. When she took his hand, her fingers small but firm in his, he helped her to her feet. "I acted without thought," he continued, his words rehearsed but sincere, "and have had my error pointed out."

The captain's fear wasn't of the woman before him, it was of the man behind her.
Rhyslin stood motionless, his expression unreadable, but his eyes— those eyes burned like the reflection of stormlight in obsidian.

Every soldier in the hall could sense the contained violence in that stillness. If his *bhannaichean* refused the apology, there would be no words, only the swift finality of judgment.

Ria, still holding the captain's hand, glanced from him to Rhyslin. [*If I don't forgive him, what happens?*]

Through the bond, there was only silence — deep and unyielding. Then she looked again, and in that stillness, she saw the answer written across his face. [*I will challenge him to a duel, and I will win.*]

She felt the calm certainty of his will ripple through their connection, and a tremor ran down her spine.

The captain felt it too, that invisible weight of power pressing on him like a descending storm.

He dared a look around, his heart sinking as he noticed the *Hin I-Balanath* delegation seated in the visitor's benches, their faces grim and armed hands resting on sword pommels. His stomach twisted. He had not insulted a servant, he had nearly sparked a diplomatic catastrophe.

He swallowed hard, turned back to Ria, and offered a half-smile that looked more like surrender than charm.

Unaware of his panic, Ria stood in quiet turmoil. Her heart thudded painfully beneath her ribs. She didn't want anyone hurt because of her, least of all by Rhyslin's hand. She caught his gaze again, her pulse quickening.

She wished she could ask Allanagh or Mayana for counsel, but decorum chained her to this moment.

[*How badly do I want him hurt?*] she wondered, biting her lower lip until the taste of copper bloomed.

And then, a whisper at the back of her mind. A gentle pulse that wasn't hers.

[*Good Goddess— is this what it feels like to communicate through the bond?*]

[*Rowena?*] she sent, startled. The Seeress had never reached out this way before.

[*Yes,*] came the soft reply, like the brush of wind through leaves. [*Are you okay?*]

[*I am fine, I suppose,*] Ria projected, her breath catching. [*I have to decide whether or not to forgive him.*]

[*I'd help you if I could,*] Rowena's tone was warm but resigned, [*but Rhyslin has a way of— well, you know.*]

Ria felt the faint ghost of a laugh and sighed aloud. [*Thank you for trying to help.*]

Drawing a slow, steadying breath, she looked up at the captain. Her voice carried clearly across the hall. "You are forgiven, Captain."

The words fell like the easing of a bowstring. The captain sagged in visible relief. "Thank you, Lady Ilyriatri," he said, his tone almost reverent. "Allow me to show you to your seat."

He moved as if the very air might break beneath him.

But before he could take two steps, Rhyslin's voice cut across the space, soft, level, but heavy as thunder before rain.

"Captain, are you trying to insult me now?"

The man froze mid-step.

"Ilyriatri is not a visitor," Rhyslin continued, his tone measured, each word sharp as flint. "She's a member of my house. Their seats are behind mine."

The captain stammered an apology, his complexion turning pale beneath the torchlight. He adjusted course instantly, leading Ria toward Rhyslin's private box, where the rest of his *bhannaichean* waited in composed silence.

As they passed, Flur's blade whispered back into its sheath, and the murmuring crowd dared to breathe again.

"What the frell is this shit?"

A harsh voice split the air, cutting through the murmuring crowd.

Rana's head snapped toward the sound, just in time to see a young man hurl something toward Rowena. Instinct overrode thought. The spellblade sprang forward, her boots scraping against polished marble as she thrust herself between the seeress and the oncoming object.

Her fingers closed around it midair. The impact jarred her arm, but she landed lightly, knees bending to absorb the force. In her hands gleamed a glass sphere the size of a skull, its interior churning with slow, smoky motion like trapped mist.

Brows lifting, she called clearly, "Maighstir Rhyslin."

Rhyslin turned immediately, his dark cloak whispering against the stone.

Rana raised the sphere so that the torchlight shimmered along its cloudy surface. "Someone was trying to hit Rowena with this."

The *draoidh's* eyes flicked from the orb to Rowena, whose expression was pale shock, then back to Rana.

His tone was calm, almost conversational, yet carried the weight of command.

"About my earlier instructions."

When Rana inclined her head, he added, "Disregard them."

She nodded once, turned sharply toward the benches, and let her voice ring out, firm and cutting: "Maighstir, are all the men in this country bullies and cowards?"

The words dropped like a gauntlet. A hush rippled through the council hall, whispers dying, movement stilled. Every eye turned toward her.

Holding their attention, she lifted the glass sphere high so that its smoky light shimmered across her face.

"One of your soldiers threw this at Lady Rowena."

A deep, weathered voice answered from the dais. "That's an accusation that could get a person killed, young lady."

Rana half-turned. The speaker was an older man, silver-haired and hard-eyed, his bearing unmistakably martial. From the insignia at his throat, two interlocked five-pointed stars, she knew him for one of the founding families.

"May I see the object?" he asked.

Rana held it aloft again, the sphere's cloudy core catching and refracting the chamber's light. The general studied it, then shook his head slowly. "Who threw it?"

She turned back toward the gallery, scanning the rows of young soldiers.

Her gaze moved methodically over their faces until she spotted the smirking one, a lieutenant with a single silver bar gleaming on his collar. She pointed. "There, sir."

"Which one, young lady?" the general pressed, voice patient but commanding.

Rana exhaled sharply, her eyes narrowing. Then she extended her finger toward the culprit and whispered, *"Nochdadh a nis cionta aon duine, cuairticheadh solus e, a thilg am ball-criostail[11]."*

---

[11] Now reveal the guilty one — let light surround him, the one who threw the crystal ball.

At her words, the air shimmered, and a figure near the back row flared with a ring of pale, silver fire that danced harmlessly over his skin.

A collective murmur rose. The general's eyes followed the glow. "What have you to say for yourself, Lieutenant Sparhawk?"

The young man stiffened, caught off guard but masking it behind contempt. "I have no idea what you are talking about, sir!" he called down, his tone brittle with defiance.

"This young lady has accused you of trying to hit Lady Rowena in the head with that crystal ball," the general said, his voice echoing up the hall.

"She's lying, General Oberon — like most of her kind."

The insult hit like a slap. Rana felt the Hin I-Balanath delegation around her bristle as one. Her hand tightened around the sphere. For a moment she hesitated, then turned toward Rhyslin.

He was already watching her. His expression unreadable, he gave the smallest of nods. Permission.

She faced Sparhawk again. "I am no liar. I have the proof here. Since the lieutenant has insulted me, I challenge him to a duel."

Sparhawk barked a laugh. "Get stuffed, girlie. I don't accept your challenge." His smirk carried the lazy arrogance of one who had never been held accountable.

Without flinching, Rana turned her head toward Rhyslin again. "You said that the men in this country had honor. I don't see it," she said coolly, raising the sphere above her head. Then she glanced at Ria, her expression softening with apology. "Do we want to live among liars and cowards?"

Ria's lips parted, unsure whether to answer. Watching her daughter, she understood: Rana wasn't provoking for vanity, she was defending her kin, their dignity, their name.

Rhyslin's eyes never left the scene. When Sparhawk turned away again, the *draoidh* spoke quietly, his voice finding the general. "General Oberon."

The older man looked up at him immediately.

"Officers in the Military have taken an oath to always tell the truth, correct?"

"Unless something changed in the last officer's class, that is correct," Oberon replied, glancing sharply toward the lieutenant. "He's not one of my officers. He must belong to another unit."

Scanning the assembly, he spotted a figure near the rear. "Colonel Oborgoff!"

The colonel, a broad-shouldered man with dark hair going grey at the temples, made his way forward. "Yes, General Oberon?"

"Get four men and make us a ten-foot ring. We have a challenge."

Oborgoff's jaw tightened, but he nodded briskly, gesturing for nearby soldiers to move.

Boots thudded and chairs scraped harshly across marble as a rough circle took shape at the center of the hall.

The colonel glanced back. "What about young Sparhawk? He didn't sound like he was going to accept the challenge."

"He doesn't have a choice. He's a lieutenant in the military." Oberon's tone was iron. His gaze locked on the glowing figure above. "Lieutenant Sparhawk, get down here."

The lieutenant's shoulders went rigid. He turned slowly, his arrogance wavering. "Yes, sir?"

"Do you intend to answer this young lady's challenge?"

"No, I do not," he said coldly. "She's a prey species and not worth considering."

The word *prey* hung like smoke in the air.

Rhyslin stepped forward from the shadows behind Oberon, his voice smooth but laced with danger. "Prey species? Nobody calls Hin I-Balanath a prey species, except for *luchd-fiadhaich.*[12] of the far northern plains." His eyes fixed on the young man. "What brings one of you into the Saorsa?"

"It's not a secret," Sparhawk said, trying to recover his composure. "My people banished me, and I came here to live. I joined the Blackhawks six years ago."

Rhyslin listened in silence, nodding once. *Such is the Saorsa,* his tone implied, a land where even exiles

---

[12] savages of the wilderness

could serve with honor. "Why did you throw that orb at my *bannaichean*?"

The lieutenant's shrug was insolent. "I was throwing the orb at the prey species, not your seeress. She just got in the way."

A low murmur rippled through the chamber.

Rhyslin looked to Oberon, who answered with a single curt nod. The general's voice cut through the tension like a blade. "I don't care why you did it, Lieutenant Sparhawk. As an officer, you will accept the challenge, fight the young lady, and fight with all of your heart."

Sparhawk's mouth twisted. "Against a prey species?"

Rhyslin's reply was soft but absolute. "Against a prey species."

Rana's jaw clenched at the repeated slur, but Rhyslin's calm steadied her.

The lieutenant's deeply tanned skin darkened further with anger. "Very well, General. I will do this and teach this young woman a lesson she won't forget," he said as he shoved through the gathered crowd toward the forming ring.

The sound of boots, drawn breath, and shifting marble filled the silence, the hall itself holding its breath as justice prepared to unfold.

The council hall rang with the grating scrape of marble chairs being dragged aside. The sound echoed up into the high, vaulted ceiling, where beams of sunlight filtered through stained glass, scattering fractured rainbows over the polished black-and-white tiles. Dust motes drifted lazily in the air, illuminated in those shafts of light. The scent of hot stone and oil from the torches mixed faintly with the metallic tang of tension.

When the last chair had been moved, a perfect circle about fifteen feet wide gleamed in the center of the chamber, a makeshift arena amid a sea of order and ceremony.

Rana stepped forward, her boots making a soft *click* on the marble floor. She moved to one edge of the circle with quiet confidence, the hem of her cloak whispering behind her. Across from her, Lieutenant Sparhawk stood rigid, a predator measuring his prey. He flexed his hands, testing the weight of them, and the muscles in his neck coiled like a drawn bowstring.

Rana held the glass orb in her right hand. Light from the stained windows shimmered within it, smoky tendrils twisting through the crystal sphere as though alive.

Sparhawk loosened the sword at his side, letting it fall back into its sheath with deliberate arrogance.

The motion said everything his smirk didn't: *this will be quick.*

"I hope you both are ready," Oberon said, his voice carrying the deep timbre of command. His eyes moved first to the girl.

"The young lady."

"Vuureona Seilmatt, daughter of Ilyriatri." The spellblade inclined her head slightly, hazel eyes calm and alert.

"Vuureona has accused you, Sparhawk, of the plains, of throwing a glass orb at Lady Rowena." The general's voice carried easily across the chamber, measured and precise. "You have denied this and called her a liar." His gaze flicked to the lieutenant, then back to Rana. "She has challenged you to a duel. As the challenged, you get to select the weapon and victory terms."

The lieutenant straightened, pride radiating from every line of him. "I won't need a weapon to beat this girl. Unarmed, to first blood," he said coolly, the confidence in his tone drawing a few low murmurs from the crowd.

Rana shrugged, still holding the orb. The smoky swirl inside pulsed faintly as though it sensed her resolve. "Agreed, unarmed and to first blood."

A low hush settled over the room. Oberon raised one hand, his expression carved from granite. "Fight."

The word struck the air like a hammer.

Sparhawk lunged first, the sound of his boots exploding against the stone, his breath harsh. His eyes locked on Rana's throat. He was fast, but she was faster. With a smooth, fluid motion, Rana dropped the orb, caught it deftly on her boot, and flicked it upward in a glittering arc.

"Briseadh agus sgaoileadh, bhuail an ceann[13]," she whispered.

The orb burst midair with a sharp, crystalline crack. Light flashed white and blinding as it shattered, spraying a cloud of glass shards that caught the sunlight like sparks from a forge. The fragments sliced across Sparhawk's face and arms in a rain of glinting pain. He cried out, staggering, crimson streaks blooming where the glass had touched skin.

Rana moved before he could recover. She ducked under his wild swing, her braid snapping behind her as she rolled to one side. Her palms brushed the cool marble; her heartbeat was calm, controlled.

Sparhawk roared in fury, spinning on his heel. His breath came in ragged bursts, the air filled with the sound of his boots and the metallic scent of blood. He charged again, blind with rage.

"Enough, Lieutenant!" Oberon's voice thundered across the hall, but Sparhawk didn't stop.

---

[13] Break and scatter—strike the head

"Stand down!" The second command went ignored, the young man's fury had drowned reason.

Then the air itself thickened, magic coiling around him in visible bands of light. A hum vibrated through the marble floor as the lieutenant froze, his limbs locked by unseen force. Sparks danced briefly across his arms like a web of lightning.

"That will be enough, Lieutenant," Oberon snapped, his patience gone. "The duel is over; you've lost."

Sparhawk blinked, his confusion cutting through the fog of anger. "Wait, what?" His voice came out hoarse, breathless.

Rhyslin stepped forward, calm and composed. "Check your face."

The lieutenant raised a trembling hand to his cheek. His fingers came away smeared with blood. The sight drained what little defiance remained in him.

He turned toward Rana, disbelief and humiliation warring across his features. "Why didn't you tell me you were a spellblade?"

Rana straightened, brushing her fingers through her hair. Her expression was level, her voice unshaken. "You didn't ask. Besides, would it have made a difference?"

Sparhawk looked at her for a long moment before sighing. "No, it wouldn't have," he admitted. "Though it might have made me act more carefully."

He accepted a towel from a nearby soldier and pressed it to his face. "I don't suppose you know how to heal, do you?"

Rana shook her head. "No, sir. I haven't gotten that far in my studies."

He nodded once, wincing as he dabbed at a fresh cut. Before he could speak again, a soft, almost melodic voice broke the silence.

"I can heal you," Flur said as she stepped forward. Her golden hair caught the sunlight, gleaming like molten metal. "If it doesn't offend you to have a prey species stop the bleeding."

A faint ripple of laughter moved through the onlookers, tension breaking like ice. Sparhawk's jaw worked for a moment before he grumbled, "I stand corrected; your tribes are anything but prey species." He lowered the towel and inclined his head stiffly. "Very well, you may heal me."

Flur's smile was faint, her tone gentle but edged with irony. She lifted a hand, tracing slow, deliberate motions in the air. "If it please thee, Mathair Astinmah," she murmured, "please heal this wounded soldier."

A warm, floral scent spread through the hall as her magic took hold. A soft gold light radiated from her fingers, flowing across Sparhawk's skin. One by one, the cuts sealed, leaving only the faintest silvery traces of their passage.

"There are a few scars," she said softly as the light faded, "but then, I've heard that plainsmen wear scars as badges of honor."

Sparhawk touched his face gingerly, feeling the smoothness where blood had once run. "We do indeed," he said quietly.

"We use them to remember life lessons that we should already know. For instance, I should have known not to pick a fight with a spellblade."

Flur's laugh, bright and musical, rippled through the air like birdsong. Around them, the hall finally exhaled, tension dissolving into murmured approval and uneasy admiration.

The duel was finished. Honor restored.
And in the shimmer of scattered glass and the lingering warmth of divine light, peace settled once more over the council hall.

Chapter Eleven

Of Dragons and New Kin

The council hall settled back into symmetry: chairs returned to their squares on the vast black-and-white floor, papers restacked, cloaks straightened. Sunlight poured through the stained glass high above, casting slow rivers of color over marble and steel. The faint smell of lamp oil mingled with cool stone and parchment; somewhere, a hinge sighed as a door eased shut.

Rhyslin and Oberon took their places at the dais, the two men framed by the ten older chairs like sentinels of an earlier age. The murmur of voices dwindled as freeholders reclaimed their seats. After five silent minutes, Rhyslin inclined his head toward the General.

Oberon raised his gavel. A small pulse of power, Rhyslin's doing, tightened the air, and the single knock struck like a bell, resonant enough to reach the farthest bench. Even the motes in the shafts of light seemed to pause.

Oberon waited until the last shuffle stilled and then began, his voice unhurried but ironbound. "Gentlemen, we are here today for two reasons." The hall drew itself inward; a hush closed like a clasp. Within moments, it was so quiet a pin might have sounded like a chisel on stone.

"Our first order of business is to inform you of the continued An fheadhainn a thuit and Orcan attacks." He drew a crystal from his jacket pocket, pale, many-faceted, and set it into the pedestal's waiting cup.

The air above his head trembled. Light climbed the crystal's heart and unfolded into a shimmering map of the Saorsa, lines of river and road traced in lambent silver. Five border points flared, each ringed by notations, troop marks, numbers, terse sigils denoting losses. "As you can see, there have been five incursions by mixed Orcan, An fheadhainn a thuit, and Ogren forces. Our forces proved superior in two battles and killed the invaders to the last man. It was a draw in two, and there were no survivors on either side in the last two." He indicated two dimmer marks within the borders. "Local Patrols have come across small bands of

Orcan and An fheadhainn a thuit that have raided small villages. We haven't been able to take any of the invaders alive, so we don't know what their plans are."

A chair creaked; a landowner rose, throat cleared against the silence. "That doesn't bode well. What does the council want us to do?"

Oberon's jaw set as he surveyed the glowing borders. "If possible, increase the patrols around your local area, keep watch for groups of strangers, and protect your local civilian populace." His finger traced the arc of incursions. "Pass along any information that you come across. We don't know why the Fallen or Orcan are working together or their end goal, but we are guessing it's not good for us."

"Is the council going to assist locals with creating their patrol squads?"

Rhyslin lifted two fingers, permission to add. Oberon nodded. Rhyslin stood, cloak falling into quiet lines.

"If the council doesn't have the funds to assist you, I will help where I may," he said, pointing to two brighter marks. "San Ang should have almost a company at the

Garrison." The draoidh pointed at the other one. "That one is near Trieste." He looked over the crowd, eyes moving like shadow over water. "I'm going to side with General Oberon when he says report on groups of strangers. Don't engage them unless you have parity or better. We don't want needless deaths on our hands."

Agreement moved through the freeholders like a windless ripple, nods, a few clipped murmurs. From the center aisle, another voice rose. "Is it true that you faced down an Ogren?"

Rhyslin inclined his head toward the speaker. "That's correct, Captain Vonze. I did capture and interrogate an Ogren." He weighed a heartbeat, then chose openness. "The Ogren in question had been dispatched to destroy Gearastan nan Trì Aibhnichean and enslave the Hin I-Balanath residents and their Queen, who was visiting. He also gave the name of the man who had sent him."

"Well, don't keep us in suspense." A nameless landowner called out. "Who sent them?"

The Draoidh looked to Oberon; a small nod answered. Rhyslin's voice stayed level. "The Mastermind of the raid is known as Saldren Halber Drache."

The hall erupted, breaths sucked in, whispers fired like sparks: *A half-drake?* "A half-drake?" and "I thought all the draches and half-drakes were dead."

The crystal map flickered slightly, as if the word itself disturbed the image.

Rhyslin let the talk crest and break, then lifted his hand. Silence settled again. "Until recently, we thought that all the drakes were dead. As for Drachen, there are only four of whom we know are still alive. One is a gold who lives in the old empire, one is a black who lives in the far northern lands, the third is a female green who is in hiding, and the fourth is a plane-traveling Skellet-Drache. His whereabouts are unknown."

A susurrus of speculation swelled, names, old tales, border rumors. Oberon and Rhyslin sat like twin stones in a fast stream, letting the current run. When at last the noise ebbed, a single figure rose, the same captain who earlier had worn his shame like a fresh bruise.

"Thank you for telling us about the invaders and the Drachen," he said to Oberon, then, steadier: "You had something else to tell us. What was it?"

The general gestured toward Rhyslin. "Maighstir Darkblade wants to discuss bringing three Hin I-Balanath clans into the Saorsa as full citizens."

The captain's gaze shifted: first to the women behind Rhyslin, then to the Hin I-Balanath in the visitor's front row. Color drained from his face. "By Mixcoatl," he whispered, "I have a feeling that I've insulted all three clans." He turned, stiff with realization, to Ria. "Haven't I?"

Rhyslin answered before the sting could spread. "Yes, You have." He held the plainsman's eyes, not unkindly. "Do you have an objection to them joining the Saorsa?"

The Captain's shoulders lowered; he sank into his chair, hands covering his face. "No, I have no objection to them joining the Saorsa."

The atmosphere softened, some pity, some approval. Rhyslin rose into that quiet and addressed the hall. "After I introduce the head of the clans, the floor may ask questions. When all questions have been answered, we will vote on their admission to the Saorsa."

He turned to the benches, voice becoming ceremonial. "Representing the Clann na Beinne, Silas falt Airgid." The silver-haired elder stood; light caught his hair like frost on steel, and he offered a grave half-bow. Rhyslin indicated the second statesman. "Representing the Clann na Coille, Sloan Sealgair sgàile." The spymaster's nod was short, eyes unreadable. "Finally, representing the Clann an Fhàsaich, Makar Lann Neimh." The elder desert-born rose with measured dignity and gave a formal bow.

Rhyslin waited for the last fold of cloth to settle. "The floor may now question the applicants."

Hands rose, dozens, a forest of questions. Rhyslin settled back, a wry breath escaping him. "The floor is yours, Oberon."

"Of course it is," the general grumbled, though the corner of his mouth twitched. He scanned the chamber and pointed. "What is your question, Maighstir De Vais?"

A younger freeholder stood, palms smoothing a lapel that didn't need it. "What skills do these people bring with them?" Sloan leaned toward Makar, voice too soft to carry. "I think you should take this, old friend."

Makar rose. His hands were roughened by sun and sand, but his voice carried like water in a cistern. "My clan has extensive knowledge of water preservation and conservation. We know how to raise crops using a minimum of water and which plants to harvest to make medicines." He tipped his head toward his companions.

"The Clann na Coille are excellent hunters and trackers and have extensive knowledge of the trees and herbs, while the Clann na Bienne can guide people through the caverns under the mountains and hunt the denizens of the high peaks." His gaze moved from face to face, unflinching. "We are an industrious people and do not shirk from battle."

A glint of humor warmed his tone. "As you have seen, even our women aren't afraid to fight when needed."

"Some of us have found that out the hard way," DeVais said with a chuckle. Laughter loosened the hall's tight seams.

Questions flowed for hours, on law, on trade roads, on oath-binding; on winter stores and levy terms and temple rights. Makar, Sloan, and Silas answered in turns, their words a braid of mountain, forest, and desert.

The crystal map dimmed and brightened as the sun wheeled; by the time Oberon tapped his gavel again, the light through the windows had shifted from white to honey.

"Let's get a show of hands for the three Hin I-Balanath clans joining the Saorsa."

Arms lifted across the grid of chairs, shadowed, then lit as the stained light moved. Clerks counted in murmurs. Out of one hundred forty-four freeholders, one hundred fifteen rose in favor; twenty held against; nine hands hovered, abstaining.

When the tally was set, Oberon stood, his voice formal and carrying. "By a majority vote, the Clann na Coille, Clann an Fhasiach, and Clann na Beinne are hereby welcomed to the Soarsa na rointean Mora as full citizens and independent states." He turned and saluted Sloan, Silas, and Makar. "Welcome to the Saorsa."

A breath the hall had been holding seemed to release. The crystal map slowly faded; the last glimmer along the borders lingered like embers. Rhyslin let his hands rest on the rail, feeling, for a moment only, the strange twinness of the day: shadow massing on the edges, and in the center, new kin bound by oath.

✦ ✦ ✦

When Rhyslin stepped out of the council hall, the sunlight caught the silver threads in his hair and haloed them in gold. The air outside was warm and clean, washed by a faint breeze from the river that wound through the capital below. The heavy wooden doors shut behind the delegation with a deep, echoing thud that seemed to close the weight of the morning's politics firmly away.

Rhyslin glanced upward, squinting past the ornate gables toward the pale sky. By his reckoning, it was just past the second hour after noon. The heat pressed gently on his shoulders, a comfortable contrast to the hall's cold marble. He turned toward the others, his expression softening.

"Would our new citizens like to get something to eat? I know of a decent place to dine," he said as he watched each of them.

The elder *hin i-Balanath* raised a hand to shield his eyes, the gold rings on his fingers catching the light. "A light meal would be nice. I don't think I've ever been questioned for so long about anything," Makar said, blinking against the sun's brilliance. He looked toward Sloan and Silas. "What do you gentlemen think?"

Silas glanced at Mayana, who smiled with calm grace. "We could use something. It's been a while since breakfast."

"What do you think, Lanna?" Sloan asked, turning to his bond.

The silver-haired woman rubbed her stomach sheepishly. "I could eat. I am a bit hungry," she admitted. "I was too nervous to eat this morning." Her stomach growled in confirmation, and she blushed, her hand half-hiding her face.

Sloan's mouth twitched with a suppressed grin before he turned to Rhyslin. "It would seem that we are in your hands, Rhyslin." Unlike Makar, he could not yet call him *old friend,* and *Maighstir* or *Mac Draoidheachd* felt too formal between equals.

"You'll like the food," Rhyslin assured them as he started down the hill. The cobbled path curved in lazy spirals between terraces of stone and ivy. "It's one of the oldest restaurants in the Capital, and the chef is an old friend of mine."

The group followed him down the slope toward the heart of the city. The afternoon light turned the white façades to amber and silver. Below them, the capital stirred, merchants calling out prices in the marketplace, distant hooves on paving stones, the mingled scent of bread, spice, and river wind. The delegation of *Hin I-Balanath* walked slower than the locals, drinking in every detail.

"For such a young country, your people make great use of classical architecture," Makar observed, studying a nearby arcade. Its columns were fluted and carved with vines and birds so lifelike they seemed ready to take flight. "This wouldn't be out of place in *Caisteal Beanntan Uaine* or the old empire, I would guess."

"It may be a young country," Rhyslin replied, "but most of the oldest freeholders came from other places. Some of them even came from the old frontier marches." As he spoke, Rana lingered behind, eyes wide with wonder. "Some, such as Marcus and I, briefly lived in the old Empire."

Makar smiled faintly, shading his eyes again. "I figured as much, old friend." His gaze followed Rana as she ran her fingers along a column's scalloped surface, the stone still cool beneath her hand. "It speaks highly of your people that they admire beauty." His grin turned sly. "How long have you known this chef of whom you speak so highly?"

Rhyslin laughed, the sound light and genuine. "I've known him since he first moved to the Saorsa. He worked for me for almost ten years as a cook."

As they neared the merchant quarter, the streets widened. The soundscape changed, from the formal hush of the upper district to the rhythmic life of trade.

Carriages rattled past. Laughter and the hiss of street vendors filled the air.

The buildings grew grander, façades layered with painted reliefs of sea nymphs and hunters, their stone patched with newer brickwork where time had left its mark.

Allanagh and Mayana exchanged knowing glances before the mountain-born bhanna spoke. "How long has this quaint little eatery been around?"

Sloan quirked an eyebrow, and she smiled at his look. "Look at the buildings, *Mo Chridhe*. They have been here a long time, and most have new construction to make them larger." She pointed to a nearby building where fresh mortar met weathered stone.

"You have a good eye," Rhyslin admitted. "Gerald bought the building twenty years ago and has added to it as he gained more business."

Allanagh chuckled softly. "What little knowledge I have comes from helping Mayana with the additions to the castle. Someone had to vet the tradesmen and check over the work." Her eyes roved the street. "What else is down here?"

Rhyslin shrugged, his cloak catching a breeze scented faintly with roasting chestnuts. "It may have changed, but the last time I was here, there were clothing stores, a haberdasher, two bookbinders, and a few general stores."

"Excellent," Mayana exclaimed. "We can do some shopping after lunch."

Makar leaned closer to Rhyslin with a conspiratorial grin. "Rhyslin, my old friend, is there a place where we may sit and enjoy a drink while our women try to buy out the stores?"

Ria's laughter rang clear as a bell, warm and affectionate. Even Rana smiled, glancing between them all, the tension of the day dissolving into shared humor.

Rhyslin's eyes glinted. "Yes, there is a place where we gentlemen may wait. My friend has an upstairs room where like-minded gentlemen may share drinks and smoke pipes while their women shop."

Sloan tilted his head, quick on the uptake. "Is this the same friend that owns the restaurant?"

"The very one," Rhyslin said, reaching for Ria's hand. Her fingers twined with his as they crossed the threshold into the café. The scent of baking bread and herbs drifted outward to greet them, and the sound of quiet laughter and clinking glasses welcomed them like an old song.

They were greeted by a six-foot-tall, dark-skinned plainsman whose easy grace matched the strength in his shoulders. He wore a crisp white shirt and black trousers tucked into soft leather boots, a wide apron tied at his waist. The faint aroma of roasted herbs and woodsmoke clung to him like a badge of pride.

"Rhyslin, *seann charaid,* it is a pleasure to see you again."

Rhyslin's face broke into a genuine smile.

The old Draoidh clasped the restauranteur's hand in both of his own, the sound of their handshake echoing faintly in the low murmur of the dining room. "Gerald, it has been far too long." His smile deepened, warm as the hearthfire beyond. "Business is going well; I take it."

Gerald's dark eyes glimmered with humor. "It is, especially the gentleman's refuge upstairs," he whispered conspiratorially, leaning closer with a grin. Then his gaze swept past Rhyslin and widened at the sight of the entourage behind him. "How many seats do you require?"

The Draoidh inclined his head, his tone easy but respectful. "Enough for my house and my guests," he said, gesturing to the people gathered behind him.

The restauranteur's smile broadened as his eyes roamed over the group, the distinct bearing of the Hin I-Balanath unmistakable even to one who'd never set foot on the plains. "Welcome to *Solas na Saorsa,*" he said, bowing deeply. "It's an honor to host members of the three clans."

The scents of honeyed wine, baked bread, and simmering meat drifted through the air as Gerald turned toward the open floor. "Would you prefer to eat in private or among the crowd?" His sharp gaze caught Makar's noncommittal shrug, Silas's thoughtful caution, and Sloan's subtle scan of the public tables. Reading them with practiced ease, Gerald nodded. "I have a private dining room large enough to accommodate you."

When Rhyslin nodded, Gerald gestured gracefully toward the far side of the restaurant. "Follow me, please."

The crowd in the common room parted instinctively as they passed. Gerald's experienced eyes noted how the large group divided into natural clusters: the golden-haired forest-born woman and the dark-haired desert-born woman on either side of Rhyslin, each slipping a hand into his. The glow in their eyes left no doubt that both were bound to him by more than loyalty. Behind them walked the younger *Teine*-born and another desert-born woman, quieter but watchful, moving with the rhythm of kinship rather than command.

He arched a brow as he studied them. The resemblance between the younger woman and the older one was striking, mother and daughter, surely.

The others followed close behind: a red-haired mountain-born woman slipping her arm around the white-haired man's side with gentle familiarity, and a silver-haired forest-born moving at pace with a tall, black-clad figure whose silence spoke of both power and restraint.

Only one man stood slightly apart, the older, silver-haired desert-born, his dignity shadowed by a quiet melancholy that made him seem lonelier amid the laughter of friends.

"Makar, why don't you join us?" the older desert-born woman said kindly, reaching out her hand.

"Thank you, Ilyriat— er, Ria, that's most gracious of you," Makar said fondly as he joined them, his voice carrying the softened rasp of age and gratitude.

Gerald smiled inwardly as he led the way to the back. The polished wood floor creaked softly beneath his boots, and conversation from the main room faded to a hum of contentment and clinking glass. He caught the lilting cadence of Rhyslin's *bannaichean,* their voices overlapping in gentle teasing, the tone rich with affection. The young Hin I-Balanath stayed silent, but the tenderness in her gaze made Gerald certain she was family.

At the far wall, he paused before a heavy oak door framed by carved ivy and brass fittings polished to a gleam. Shaking his head fondly at his own nostalgia, he drew a key from his apron and unlocked it with a satisfying click. Warm lamplight flickered within, and the faint smell of polished wood and wine drifted out.

"Feel free to sit anywhere," he said, stepping aside and watching as they entered the thirty-foot room. Its walls were paneled in rich mahogany, carved with interlaced knotwork and soft bas-reliefs of trees and riverbanks. Golden light spilled from brass sconces, catching in the silver hair of the Hin I-Balanath and in the soft highlights of Ria's dark braid.

"Wasn't this table upstairs the last time I was here?" Rhyslin asked, lowering himself into a seat at the largest table, a magnificent piece carved from a single mahogany trunk, its surface polished to a mirror sheen.

"Yes, sir, it was," Gerald replied, pride glinting in his tone. "I moved it down here when I opened this room. I'm pleased that you noticed."

He waited until everyone had chosen their seats, the laughter of the women, the low murmur of men settling into chairs, then clasped his hands. "What would you like me to cook?"

Rhyslin looked around the table, meeting each gaze, then nodded once. "We'll leave it up to you."

To say Gerald was ecstatic was an understatement. His face lit up as though he'd just been handed a festival feast. "Very good, *Maighstir Darkblade*," he said, and with a grateful look, he slipped back toward the kitchen.

◆ ◆ ◆

The kitchen was alive with the rhythm of craft—the hiss of oil, the crackle of flame, the scent of thyme and seared venison.

"I saw you taking Darkblade to the private dining room," said his partner, Jesin, leaning against the doorframe, wiping his hands on a towel. "Did he say what they wanted?"

"Rhyslin said we could fix them whatever we wanted," Gerald answered, still breathless from excitement.

Jesin's grin widened. "His guests are Hin I-Balanath from all three clans."

"So, a light meal with bites of meat instead of chunks," Jesin mused. "Three courses: a light salad for the first, followed by bread, cheese, and lightly cooked meat.”

“Perfect,” Gerald said, already pulling ingredients from the shelves. The scent of fresh greens and smoked salt filled the room. “Dessert?”

“How about some plum pudding?”

“That sounds perfect,” Gerald agreed. “Do we have three bottles of Brandywine?”

From the far end of the kitchen, their assistant, Merilon, raised his head. “We have a crate in the cellar. Would you like me to get it?”

When the two cooks nodded, the young man vanished through the swinging door.

Time passed, too long for comfort. Gerald, ever the perfectionist, began pacing. “Where is that lad? It shouldn’t take that long to get the wine.”

Jesin, used to calming his partner, handed him a cup of cooking wine. “Unless he got injured, he’ll be here. Maybe something was wrong with the wine.”

Just then, the door swung open, and Merilon returned, slightly breathless, his sleeves dusted with sawdust and cork flecks. “The deliverymen must not have paid attention to how they stored the wine when they delivered it. I found it upside down, with two corks popped."

Gerald's eyes widened in horror.

"I ran to the vintners," Merilon continued quickly. "They apologized for the cockup and gave us two crates to replace it. They'll pick up the bad batch tomorrow."

Gerald's shoulders sagged in relief. "Bless you, lad. Remind me to give you a bonus on payday."

He took a long breath, then looked toward the door leading to the private dining room. "It's time to see if *Maighstir Darkblade* and his guests will like the meal."

Merilon grinned, unpacking the new bottles with reverence. "I'll remind you on payday." His eyes swept over the plates of delicate meats, the glistening pudding waiting for its drizzle of syrup. "Gerald, you've outdone yourself. He can't help but like it."

Still doubtful, Gerald adjusted a sprig of parsley and the placement of the bread basket. "Perfection isn't for them," he muttered. "It's for the story they'll remember."

The kitchen was alive with low firelight and the comforting clatter of dishes. The scent of roasted meat and warm bread hung in the air like a memory of home. Gerald hovered over the final platter, his dark hands fussing over a single green leaf.

"Gerald, you need to stop. If you adjust one more sprig of *lettuidh,* you'll mangle it." Jesin said with a grin. The younger cook leaned against the counter, arms crossed, a faint smudge of flour on his sleeve. "It can't get any more perfect. Let's take it out and see what they say."

Gerald froze mid-motion, then exhaled through his nose, the tension in his shoulders visible. "I don't know why I get so nervous when it comes to him," he said, trying for a confident expression but failing to hide the flicker of worry in his eyes.

"I do," Merilon said, his tone half-teasing, half-wise. "You feel that way for the same reason I do when it comes to you."

When Gerald turned, one brow raised, Merilon continued with a small, knowing smile. "You gave me my big break, just like he gave you yours. You want to show him that you've continued to improve."

Gerald blinked, the insight striking deeper than he'd expected. "Damn," he muttered, then chuckled, shaking his head. "When did you become so knowledgeable about people, Merilon?"

He stepped back from the counter, flexing his hands as if shaking off nerves. "You're right, Merilon. Thank you." He turned toward the trays. "Let's do this thing."

With quiet efficiency, the trio loaded steaming plates onto three serving carts. The smell of herbs, butter, and seared meat rose around them as they rolled the carts out of the kitchen. The hum of the dining room grew louder, laughter, silverware, and the clink of glass, until they reached the private door at the far wall.

Upon entering, Gerald paused. The private dining room glowed softly under lamplight, the polished mahogany table gleaming like dark honey. He noticed immediately that Rhyslin's party had grown, five new figures seated near the far end.

"Oh, I didn't realize that others had joined you." He offered a half-bow, his apron rustling. "If you don't mind waiting, Maighstir Marcus, Lady Tanner, we'll have your dinner fixed."

Marcus nodded graciously. "It's fine, Gerald. We surprised you." At his side, Natolie smiled, her eyes warm with apology.

Gerald hesitated, looking to Rhyslin for direction. "Would you like to wait until their meal is ready, or would you like to eat now?"

"We'll eat now," Rhyslin said with a grin. "Marcus and his party can look on as we enjoy our meal. It's what they get for not coming with us earlier."

The ranger rolled his eyes with practiced ease. "If you hadn't been in such a hurry, we would have left with you."

"You know how much I detest council meetings, even when I'm part of them," Rhyslin admitted. "Besides, I wanted to get the ladies out before something else happened." He glanced sideways at Rana and winked. "Sparhawk might have come back for a second round."

The young spellblade blushed, her fingers fidgeting with the napkin in front of her.

"And don't you start apologizing for something that wasn't your fault," Rhyslin said gently. Pride warmed his tone. "You were defending your family; there can be no greater honor than that."

Rana swallowed hard, her throat tightening as she blinked away sudden tears. The lamplight caught the sheen in her eyes, and she quickly dabbed them away before anyone could notice.

Rembran, sitting near Marcus, raised his glass in salute. "I don't know about Marcus here, but I'm proud of you," he said warmly. "You beat him without ever laying a finger on him."

"Thank you, Maighstir Rembran. That means a lot coming from you," Rana replied softly, fighting the quiver in her voice.

The cooks exchanged curious looks, catching only fragments of the exchange. Gerald finally asked, "If you don't mind my asking, who did you defeat and why?"

Rana glanced down at her plate, still collecting herself. Marcus leaned forward, taking the lead. "There's a certain Lieutenant that goes by the name of Sparhawk."

"I know of him," Gerald said, frowning slightly. "He's got unique viewpoints on what he considers to be 'prey species.'"

His gaze flicked toward the Hin I-Balanath with sympathy.

"He's not the only one," Natolie murmured under her breath, her expression shadowed by experience.

Rhyslin sighed, his voice low but steady. "No, he's not. We can't legislate how people think or act. We can only challenge their beliefs."

"So, what did Lieutenant Sparhawk do that deserved a duel?" Merilon asked tentatively. "Oh, I'm sorry — I just assumed it came to a duel."

"Nothing to be sorry about, young man," Makar said, his voice a deep rumble, kind but commanding. He leaned back, the lamplight softening his weathered features.

"The rather bigoted Lieutenant threw a crystal ball at Lady Rowena's head. Young Rana here intercepted it and called him out on it."

"He called me a liar," Rana blurted, then froze, realizing she had interrupted. Her blush deepened. "I'm sorry, General Makar."

He waved her off with a grandfatherly smile. "There's nothing to be sorry for, lass." Turning back to Merilon, he continued, "He called her a liar, and with Rhyslin's permission, she challenged him to a duel and won without laying a finger on him."

Jesin blinked in disbelief. "How did she do that? I've seen the Lieutenant. He's fast and never misses."

Makar smiled, pride crinkling the corners of his eyes. "Our young lady here is an accomplished spellblade. In his rush to defend his honor, young Sparhawk agreed to fight the match to first blood."

"Then what happened?" Gerald asked, leaning forward unconsciously, utterly absorbed.

Rhyslin chuckled, his voice warm with mischief. "Once the fight started, she drop-kicked the orb in his direction and shattered it with a spell." He smiled fondly at Rana. "The spell she used created a cone of shattered crystal focused on Sparhawk's head." He leaned back, amusement flickering across his face.

"I don't think the young Lieutenant even noticed that the shards had wounded him. He wouldn't stop, even when General Oberon called the match. It took me holding him inside an anti-kinetic bubble to stop him."

The cooks stood frozen for a heartbeat, the tale hanging in the air like a good legend. Gerald finally exhaled and said, "Somehow, I don't think that's the whole story."

"You're right," Marcus said as he sat back down at his group's chosen table. "But telling stories doesn't make lunch."

The three cooks jumped, startled back to reality. Jesin slapped a hand to his forehead. "I forgot about your group, Maighstir Tanner," he said, already turning toward the door. "We'll be right back with yours. Until then, enjoy some Brandywine, on the house."

"Don't mind if I do," Marcus said cheerfully, grabbing a bottle. The soft pop of the cork echoed through the room, followed by the glug of poured wine and the faint perfume of fruit and oak.

Natolie smiled at Gerald and his team. "If it helps, you only have to fix enough for three of us."

"Only three?" Merilon asked, looking puzzled. "But there are five of you."

"That's true," Ixa said, her copper-red hair catching the firelight as she turned. "Andros and I don't eat." She paused at their curious looks. "I'm an air elemental, and Andros is an earth elemental."

The young assistant's eyes widened in understanding. "That makes sense," he said, glancing toward Gerald.

The restauranteur nodded. "Then it will only take a few minutes to fix you three something to eat."

The door swung shut behind the cooks, leaving the murmur of voices and the sound of pouring wine. Laughter rippled through the private room, the kind that rises after long struggle, the kind that sounds like peace. Outside, the kitchen filled again with the rhythm of knives and ladles, and through the warm air drifted the scent of hope, plated and served with care.

Chapter Twelve

The Shade that Hunted in Daylight

The dining room hummed with the soft murmur of conversation and the faint clinking of glassware. Afternoon light slanted through the tall windows, golden and dappled by the shifting leaves outside. The scent of roasted lamb and herbs lingered in the air, mingled with the faint sweetness of baked bread and wine.

"You outdid yourself," Rhyslin commented when they had finished their meal, leaning back in his chair with clear satisfaction.

"Thank you, sir," Gerald said with a half-bow, pride shining in his eyes. "We are glad that you enjoyed your meal."

His hands, still faintly reddened from the heat of the kitchen, twitched as if resisting the urge to tidy something.

Ria looked up from the table and smiled warmly. "The *uan ròsta*[14] was excellent. It's been a long time since I've had one that fell off the bone."

"Yes, very. The *cearc bakte*[15] was tasty," Rowena added as she gently pushed her plate away, her tone graceful and reserved.

Flur dabbed her lips with a linen napkin and smiled contentedly. "The *iasg friogais*[16] was perfect, as were the *buntàta bakte*[17]."

Gerald and his partners exchanged triumphant looks, praise like this was rare, and in this company, priceless. The glow of satisfaction softened Gerald's usually sharp features.

Rhyslin rose, adjusting the silver clasp on his cloak. "The manse hasn't been the same without you, Gerald. The cooks are good, but they don't have your experience."

"Thank you, Maighstir Darkblade," Gerald said, bowing his head. "That means a lot to me."

---

[14] roast lamb
[15] Baked Chicken
[16] Fried Fish
[17] Baked Potatoes

Ria stood, smoothing the folds of her gown. "If you will excuse us, *mo chridhe.* I'll pay for the meal, and then we ladies will go shopping."

Rhyslin grinned, his eyes brightening with amusement. "Have fun shopping."

The group rose in a rustle of fabric and quiet laughter. As Ria and the others left, the faint jingle of the door chime marked their departure, and the scent of lavender perfume hung faintly in their wake.

After the door closed, Marcus leaned back in his chair and smirked. "Are you sure giving her access to your accounts is a good idea?"

Rhyslin raised an eyebrow, a glint of dry humor in his gaze. "Ria?" When the ranger nodded, the draoidh chuckled. "Marcus, Ria is the keeper of my finances. She knows how much I've got, where it's stored, what investments I've made, and she's helped balance the accounts."

Marcus grunted, his tone noncommittal but his grin betraying amusement. "Besides," Rhyslin continued, "I haven't seen you say no to Natolie yet."

"True," Marcus admitted with a grin, tugging on the corner of his cloak. "I can't seem to say no to her." He stood, stretching slightly after the long meal, and walked over to the draoidh. "What should we do with the afternoon?"

"You picked an opportune time to ask," Rhyslin said as he turned toward the remaining gentlemen. "I propose that we retire to the lounge upstairs and partake in some pipesmoke."

Makar rose as well, his chair scraping softly against the floor. "As much as I'd like to join you," he said with a rueful smile, "Silas, Sloan, and I need to talk to some people about purchasing land, supplies, and craftsmen." He placed a hand on Rhyslin's shoulder, the gesture warm and familiar. "Now that we are citizens, I must start planning those communities near Eola."

"I understand," Rhyslin replied, nodding with quiet approval. "Those we are placed in charge of must come first." He clasped Makar's forearm in farewell. "We'll meet you later at the Silver Moon."

As the three Hin I-Balanath departed, their heavy steps echoed faintly against the wooden floor. The air settled into a companionable calm. Rhyslin turned to Marcus and Rembran. "Shall we?"

"Of course," Marcus said, reaching into his pouch for his pipe and pouch of *tobaq.* The faint scent of dried leaves drifted up as he followed Rhyslin toward the stairs at the back of the room.

They ascended the narrow staircase, the floorboards creaking softly beneath their boots. The air grew cooler as they reached the upper floor, where the windows opened wide onto the city below.

Outside, the late sun painted the rooftops in hues of gold and copper.

Rhyslin set his staff aside and pulled out his pipe, its ivory bowl smooth from years of use.

He filled it carefully with *tobaq* leaves, the faint crackle of dried herbs breaking the silence.

"How long has it been since we've been here?" Marcus asked, glancing toward the window and the familiar skyline beyond.

"I believe it's been five years," the draoidh answered, summoning a small flame between his fingers to light his pipe. The glow briefly illuminated his face, highlighting the creases of thought at the corners of his eyes. "I think that was the last time I attended a council meeting." He extended the flame toward Marcus in a wordless offer.

The ranger leaned forward and accepted, lighting his own pipe. "That sounds about right," he said, taking a long draw and holding it before exhaling a soft ribbon of smoke. "This can't be all you've got planned for today. What do you have planned?" he asked with a conspiratorial glint in his eye.

"Well," Rhyslin said, a wry smile playing on his lips, "I need to go to the dockyards and check on the new cutter I commissioned."

A breeze drifted through the open window, stirring the smoke between them. Below, the city moved on, merchants calling, bells tolling, the hum of life continuing under the fading sun, as two old friends sat in companionable silence, sharing a moment of calm before the storm.

✦ ✦ ✦

The afternoon sun hung lazily over the capital, its golden light glancing off glass windows and cobbled streets still damp from the morning's wash. The air carried the mingled scents of baking bread, fresh-cut fabric, and the faint metallic tang of horse tack from passing carriages.

Ria and the ladies moved easily among the bustle, their arms light and unburdened, thankfully, the shopkeepers had promised to deliver their purchases directly to the Silver Moon.

They had been shopping for hours, four clothiers, two cobblers, and even a stationery supply store, each one a trove of color, scent, and texture. Silks whispered beneath their fingers; the aroma of leather and waxed thread clung to their clothes. Now, at a shaded corner where two streets crossed, they paused to rest beneath a wrought-iron lamp that clicked softly in the breeze.

Their laughter spilled like birdsong into the afternoon air, bright and carefree, at least until the conversation turned teasing. Natolie's voice, warm and sly, carried above the murmur of the crowd.

"Why the blush, young one?" she teased, leaning close enough for her perfume, a spicy blend of myrrh and rose, to swirl between them. "Are you, by chance, wishing it was you that the old draoidh was caressing, kissing, and making love to?"

Rana's cheeks flushed a fierce crimson, as though the sun itself had found her. The young hin i-balanath shifted from foot to foot, her fingers worrying the hem of her sleeve. She could feel the eyes of passersby, though they paid her no mind.

Feeling out of place, Rana wondered why she was being picked on. Her discomfort only played into the sealgair aisling's strategy, and she poked at the young woman's insecurities.

"Don't you worry," Natolie teased. "One day, you will get what you want and wonder why it took so long."

A lump rose in Rana's throat. She bit her tongue and swore to herself that she wouldn't cry, not here, not now, and not in front of Natolie.

"Stop teasing Rana, you shameless hussy," Rowena said as she stepped into the fray, her tone as sharp as the click of her heels on the cobblestone. Natolie only smiled at the seeress.

"Me, a hussy?" Natolie feigned dismay, one hand over her heart. "I am but a product of my breeding." She grinned shamelessly. "Why are you jumping to Rana's defense? She's no kin to you."

Rowena tossed her hair back over her shoulder, sunlight catching the raven-black strands. "Wrong, you purveyor of carnal desire. When I bonded with my Maighstir, these women became my teaghlach, and family always takes care of family."

Natolie conceded the verbal match with a friendly smile. "Now, whatever shall we do with the remaining two and a half uairean of our afternoon?"

The air smelled faintly of jasmine and old parchment from the nearby bookbinder's stall as Flur leaned close to Ria. Her golden hair shimmered in the light as she whispered,

"We could always go and buy some lingerie. I don't have a wide enough selection to distract Rhyslin."

Ria snorted, the sound bright and genuine. "You don't keep anything on long enough to worry about it. If

I didn't know better, I'd say you were constantly ann an teas."

Her use of the old colloquialism drew delighted laughter from Flur. Her blue eyes sparkled with mischief as she replied, "You are right about that. Rhyslin always stirs my flames."

She poked Ria in the side. "You can't deny that he doesn't do the same for you."

"Why would I deny it?" Ria shot back. "I'm happier than I've been in a long time."

The moment was warm, lighthearted, the sort of laughter that belongs to the sunlit hours before dusk. Yet in that laughter, a subtle wind began to stir: cool, dry, and unsettlingly hollow.

Natolie, overhearing a part of that conversation, couldn't resist teasing Rana again. "What would you wear to seduce Rhyslin?"

Rana blushed again, her mind betraying her. Images flooded her thoughts, herself in gauzy white, moonlight filtering through sheer fabric, Rhyslin's dark eyes upon her. The fantasy stole her breath and drew a deeper crimson to her cheeks.

Then came a different shiver. Tiny bumps danced across her skin, and the hairs on her arms prickled.

The light dimmed slightly, as though a cloud had passed over the sun, yet when she glanced upward, the sky was still blue.

Her eyes flicked to Natolie, just in time to see her summon a blade of pure shadow. The weapon pulsed faintly, its dark edge drinking in the remaining light. Natolie's stance shifted, poised, alert.

The short hair on Rana's neck stood up, warning her of danger. She slid her hand to her sword hilt, the familiar feel of leather grounding her as the world tilted toward dread.

Then the light truly died. One heartbeat they stood in a bright afternoon; the next, the world was swallowed whole. The air turned cold and still, thick as a tomb.

A voice slithered through the blackness, ancient and venomous:

My, my, what do we have here? Could it be six tasty morsels to assuage my hunger?

Each word stretched and hissed inside their skulls, bypassing their ears entirely.

The women froze. Breath caught in their throats; hearts pounded painfully in their chests. The smell of rot and cold stone seemed to ooze from nowhere, and each of them felt as though unseen fingers brushed their hair or skimmed their arms.

[Where are you, Rhyslin?] Ria's thought rang sharp and frightened across the bond.

[We are heading in your direction,] came his reply, calm but taut with urgency. [Get as far away from it as you can.]

Laughter echoed in the dark, high and broken. ***Do run, little morsels. Fear brings out the taste of your despair— One by one, I will devour you. One by one, you will fall, calling out to gods that can't help you.***

The taunting voice reverberated off unseen walls, and phantom sounds began to crawl through the black, a dragging footstep here, a whispered breath there. Somewhere to the left, a sobbing child. To the right, the sound of claws scratching stone.

Unable to bring themselves to run, the women huddled together, their backs nearly touching, the air around them alive with dread. Only Natolie's cold focus and Rana's shaking resolve held them from panic.

As the last remnants of light died, the dark pressed closer, tasting of iron and decay. Natolie's gut twisted with recognition, it felt *familiar,* though she couldn't yet name the memory that itched beneath her skin.

"Rana, can you give us some light?" she asked, voice low but steady, as the living darkness curled tighter around them like a predator preparing to strike.

✦ ✦ ✦

Rhyslin stood by the tall window, half-veiled in the smoke curling from his pipe. The late afternoon light slanted across the room in molten amber, catching on glass decanters and the polished brass of the wall sconces. Below, the city hummed softly, voices blending with the clatter of hooves, the rhythm of life unbroken.

He drew on his pipe one last time, savoring the mellow sweetness of the tobaq and the faint bite of spice at the back of his throat. Then the light dimmed. It was subtle at first, like a passing cloud, but it didn't return.

A strange hush followed, thick and absolute. The golden warmth bled from the room until all that remained was a twilight gray.

"Well, there it goes," he muttered, tapping the bowl of his pipe against the windowsill. The echo sounded muffled, as though the air itself had thickened. He reached outward with his senses, letting the flow of Draoidheachd brush against his awareness. A cold current met him, sharp and oily. "That's not good."

"No, it's not." Marcus's voice was tense, his hand already brushing the hilt of his sword. The ranger's eyes flicked to the window, where the world beyond had turned eerily still, no breeze stirred the banners, no birds crossed the sky. "By the pricking of my thumbs..."

"Indeed," the draoidh commented. He turned his pipe upside down, the last flecks of ash falling soundlessly onto the floorboards. The soft clink of metal as he slid the pipe into his pouch seemed far too loud in the growing silence.

"What are you two talking about?" Rembran asked, still wondering what was happening. The younger man looked from one to the other, his brow furrowing. "What happened to the light?"

"Something evil has this way come," Rhyslin replied, his voice calm but edged with gravity. His gray eyes glinted faintly, catching what little light remained. "Open your senses, Rembran, but be mindful of the danger."

The younger mage hesitated, then obeyed. He closed his eyes, steadying his breath, and reached outward.

The air seemed to hum around him, faintly electric, laced with whispers that weren't quite sound. The sensation crawled along his skin, cold as the touch of unseen hands.

Rembran flinched. "Oh, I see," he whispered, feeling the vast, unnatural dark pressing against the edges of perception. "What is it?"

"I do not know," Rhyslin said softly, his tone measured even as the lines deepened at the corners of his eyes. He extended his own awareness, pushing farther through the malignant haze. The darkness responded, twisting like a living thing, recoiling from his touch. "Whatever it is, it has found the ladies and is stalking them."

"We can't have that," Marcus said, his voice grim. He tapped the embers from his pipe, tucking it swiftly into the pocket of his cloak.

The faint smell of charred leaf lingered in the air as he straightened. "How are they doing?"

"They are well for the moment; however, that thing is playing upon their deepest fears," Rhyslin said, already reaching for his staff. The wood pulsed faintly beneath his fingers, resonating with the urgency in his voice.

He started toward the door, boots striking the floorboards in firm, deliberate rhythm. He knew too well how fear could paralyze, how it stripped reason and courage away until only panic remained. And he wondered, briefly, how Rana was faring under that weight.

The question would have to wait.

When Rhyslin and his companions stepped beyond the inn's heavy oak door, the change struck them like a physical blow. The air outside was thick, the darkness total.

No moon, no torch, no starlight, just a smothering black that seemed to drink the warmth from their skin. The smell of damp stone and cold iron clung to every breath.

Even the city itself felt dead. The familiar sounds, the chatter of merchants, the creak of wagon wheels, had vanished, leaving only a dull silence broken by the faint, distant moan of something not quite wind.

"We need to hurry," Rhyslin said, his voice steady though the darkness pressed in around them. He led the way down streets turned alien by shadow, the sound of their footsteps swallowed before it could echo. "Natolie won't be able to protect them for long. In fact, I fear that she's about to engage the creature."

As they quickened their pace, the draoidh's staff began to glow faintly, a soft silver shimmer fighting against the black.

The light wavered, flickered, and was gone, devoured by the malevolent dark ahead.

———————— ✦ ✦ ✦ ————————

The air was thick, heavy, almost liquid, as though the night itself had turned to tar. Every breath the women drew tasted faintly of soot and old copper. The cobblestones beneath their feet were slick with unseen moisture, and the faint scuff of their shifting boots seemed to echo too long, as if the darkness were reflecting sound back at them.

"Rana, can you gather us some light?" The question, sharp and tense, drew the spell blade from her reverie. Her fingers trembled slightly as she traced a sigil in the air, silver lines sparking into brief existence before the void swallowed them whole. She waited, one heartbeat, two, but no light bloomed.

The darkness seemed to absorb the gesture, drinking it down greedily. The faint ozone scent of spent magic lingered for a moment before fading into the oppressive black.

Rana shook her head, though she knew Natolie couldn't see her. "No. Something is preventing it." Her voice was taut, thin as a drawn wire. She tried again, this time drawing her blade with a metallic whisper, the steel gleaming faintly with its own inner light. But even that glow faltered and died, as if the sword itself feared to shine. "Whatever it is, it's more powerful than I," she explained.

The *sealgair aisling* made a rude sound under her breath, the familiar defiance in her tone barely masking her unease. "Until the men get here, we are on our own."

The silence that followed was suffocating. Then, soft, deliberate, came the sound of footsteps.

They weren't hurried or frantic; they were patient. Predatory.

From the darkness, phantom scents curled around them, stale sweat, unwashed flesh, and something fouler still, like spoiled meat. The odor clung to the back of their throats, evoking the most primal of fears.

Each woman heard the sounds differently. Ria swore she could hear low, guttural chuckles; Flur could almost feel a breath on her neck. In their minds, the voices of men whispered, threats half-formed and promises of pain.

The ancient instinct to run, to hide, clawed at their bellies.

This isn't right, Natolie thought, her heart pounding beneath the tight leather of her jerkin.

Her father's lessons came back to her, his calm voice teaching her to separate illusion from reality, fear from fact. He had been a master of deception, using trickery to unbalance his foes in battle.

And now, those same tactics whispered at the edge of her mind.

"Beware. The darkness is trying to trick us," she cautioned, her words low but steady.

"No kidding," Rana whispered, her voice trembling but controlled. She had already reached the same conclusion. Her sword arm ached from tension as she shifted her stance, back-to-back with the others. They couldn't fight what they couldn't see, and she had the sinking feeling that the phantoms were feeding on their fear, drawing strength from Flur's panic and her mother's rising dread.

Somewhere beyond the veil of black, something moved. The faint scrape of claws against stone. A breath that wasn't human.

And still, the darkness held.

The darkness pressed against them like a living thing, cold and damp, smelling faintly of rot and wet earth. Rhyslin's staff thudded softly on the cobbles as he led them, the sound sharp and too loud in the black. Lanterns down other side-streets were dead pinpricks; even the distant clatter of market life had gone mute. Each breath tasted metallic and thin.

"Rhyslin?" The ranger inquired as the draoidh unerringly led them into the darkness.

"They still yet live," was the reply from the man ahead of them. "The time approaches, in which we still might save them."

Rhyslin's steps were resolute, boots sure even where the street turned unfamiliar in shadow.

Marcus counted the steps, reaching one hundred thirty before they stopped, and he heard Rhyslin's declaration.

"Begone, abomination, your kind is not allowed here!" the draoidh said as he forced the ambient magic to dispel some of the unnatural darkness.

For a blink, the black thinned like smoke blown aside; the air stung the eyes with the scent of ozone and old rain. Beyond Rhyslin's outstretched staff, a figure resolved from the gloom. Vaguely man-sized, it watched them with an ungainly stillness. Its arms hung too long, wrists brushing knees. The cloak it wore seemed studded with a thousand tiny spheres, not jewels, but orbs of color that pulsed on their own, each throbbing to some private, sick rhythm.

The creature turned, hissing and displaying uneven rows of dagger-sharp teeth. Baleful red-gold eyes bore into the unperturbed draoidh. **Nobody can keep me from what I desire, not even you**, it boasted, suddenly turning and lunging at Natolie, who barely had time to raise her shadow blade to block the attack.

The blade passed through him as if through fog; where it should have struck, there was nothing but the faintest ripple of air. The creature cackled as her blade slid right through him, leaving no mark on his form. The sealgair aisling blinked as she carefully withdrew beyond his reach.

"Shadows cannot harm me," the creature boasted, stalking toward the redhead, who wisely kept retreating.

Rhyslin's jaw tightened. He pushed at the air with the tip of his staff again, braided threads of light trying to fight back the black.

The darkness roiled like oil, slithering against his control and pooling where his fingers had passed.

The draoidh tried once more to dispel the darkness, only to have it roil against his control. "We need to withdraw. It is preventing the use of draoidheacd," he informed his companions.

The words were grim and immediate; in that moment even the sound of their own breathing seemed loud. Marcus and Rembran drew blades that flashed briefly with a pale blue as the steel caught whatever stray light remained, and they stepped forward to form a line at Rhyslin's shoulder.

They were so intent on the creature that they were surprised when the earth beneath it heaved up and swallowed it whole. The ground shuddered; scent of wet loam and crushed root filled their noses.

"There's not much time," Andros grunted as he worked to contain the dark creature. "Even now, it works to escape my hold."

The elemental's hands were buried ankle-deep in the cobbles where the street had opened like soft soil. Mud and grit clung to his forearms as he pushed, shaping the earth into a rising dome that wrapped around the thing like a tomb. The dome steamed where the creature's cold touched hot stone.

Taking advantage of the moment, Rhyslin turned and called out to the women. "Get over here. Andros won't be able to hold it for very long."

The command cut through the fear like a blade. Without a wasted word, Ria and the other women hurried and made their escape, feet splashing in the slick street as they ran past the men and down the lane.

The smell of their perfume and the rustle of skirts vanished ahead of them.

Rana was the last to disappear before the earthen shell shattered, and the eldritch creature growled at the earth elemental.

You have deprived me of my prey! It screamed in a rage. No matter. I will feed upon your suffering and suffer you shall.

Its voice was a tearing thing, like cloth ripped across stone; the echo of it vibrated the teeth. The creature's anger blurred the air around it, filaments of darkness making and unmaking shapes that tried to slip through the cracks in Andros's prison.

"Oh, shut up," Rhyslin muttered under his breath as he fought to control the ambient power around them. The Draoidheacd he wrenched at felt viscous, sticky with whatever the thing exuded. "It's no good, I can't do a thing. It's muddied everything up."

He shook his head, disgusted by the slimy tendrils of darkness clinging to the edges of his sight. "Get to safety. I'll be right behind you."

Marcus stared at him momentarily in disbelief, then turned and made his escape, followed quickly by

Rembran. Their boots slapped the wet stones, then were gone.

When the others had made their escape, the draoidh turned to Andros. "How long can you hold it?"

"Long enough for you to get away," the elemental replied as he closed his eyes and reached into the ground. His voice was a low rumble, the sound of stone settling. "Get ready," he whispered as he buried the creature under another dome of earth.

He didn't have to tell Rhyslin when to move, for the very instant the creature was buried, the draoidh turned and ran down the street, holding his staff like a runner's baton. The sound of his steps was fierce, the staff tapping a measured rhythm on the cobbles as he fled.

"Nooooo!" The creature screamed as it shattered the earthen dome and stared at the elemental standing in its way. **I will destroy you, and then I will feed upon your friends.**

Its scream was a tearing, wet noise that left the hairs on their arms standing. The thing convulsed, sloughing darkness like a skin, and then, with a last furious snarl, it lunged for Andros.

Andros listened to its ranting and flashed a mocking grin. "Catch me if you can," he taunted as he sank into the ground and disappeared, the earth closing over him with the soft, hungry sound of a mouth shutting. The cobbles settled again, leaving a silence that rang with the aftermath of something barely contained.

Chapter Thirteen

The Shadow and the Draoidh

The common room of the Silver Moon was a haven of noise and nervous light. The hearthfire blazed like a captured sunrise, its amber glow pushing back the gloom that pressed against the windows. Shadows gathered thick at the corners of the room, and the air carried the mixed scent of damp wool, smoke, and fear. The patrons spoke in low murmurs, tankards forgotten mid-table, all ears straining toward the creak of the door each time the wind rattled it.

When they had first arrived, Ria guided the women to a table tucked in the farthest corner, a pool of candlelight ringed by darkness. She kept glancing toward the door, the muscles in her jaw tight.

Marcus and Rembran arrived moments later, dusted with ash and rain, their faces grim. Ria's relief at seeing them was tempered by the absence of one man.

It had taken Marcus only minutes to impose order on chaos. He barked instructions, sharp but calm, his voice a steady anchor in the storm of frightened whispers. Men who had stood staring blankly into their cups were suddenly useful, posted at windows, watching the street; the broadest among them stood near the doors, hands on hilts, eyes hard.

"Marcus, do you think he's okay?" Ria whispered to the ranger as she handed him a mug of water. "Why did you leave him behind?"

The ranger took the mug, his roughened fingers brushing hers. He read the worry in her eyes before answering, his tone low, patient.

"Because he told me to 'get while the getting is good,'" he explained, tapping a finger against the rim of the mug for emphasis. "He saw what I didn't. He saw that Nat's shadow blade didn't affect the creature." He sighed, setting the mug down on the scarred oak bar. "He watched Rembran try to skewer it, and it shrugged him off."

He glanced toward the entrance just as the door banged open, a gust of chill air sweeping in with a man dragging his wife and children close behind him. Their faces were pale, eyes wide as they made for the fire.

Flur, who had overheard, stepped closer and laid a comforting arm around Marcus's shoulders. "Rhyslin is the most powerful *Draoidh* I've ever seen. Why couldn't he chase it off?"

"If I had to guess," Rembran said, his expression dark as he set his mug aside, "he couldn't draw on the ambient *draoidheacd*." He grimaced. "Whatever that thing is, it can nullify *draoidheacd* over a wide area." His breath came out in a frustrated sigh. "I tried to summon a fireball and couldn't do it." The spell blade turned toward Rana. "What about you?"

She shook her head, her voice small but steady. "I tried to gather light and couldn't even feel it." Rana rubbed her forearms, chasing away the ghostly chill of memory. "It was like someone had thrown a wet blanket over a campfire. It just wasn't there."

Marcus looked to Natolie, who met his gaze evenly. "I managed to summon my shadow blade. I couldn't even scratch it. I think it's from a shadow plane."

She paused as the door opened again, letting in two drenched men who hurried to the hearth and crouched near the flames. "I think it hunts women."

A few patrons turned toward her at that, unease flickering like the firelight across their faces.

"It'll be okay. If anyone can survive, it's Rhyslin," Marcus said, though his gaze lingered on the door. "Andros stayed behind as well. I wonder why."

"I know why," came Ixa's voice from behind them, smooth and amused, her tone a ripple of wind through silk. Her lips curved in a knowing smile, as though she'd been listening for the question.

Ria spun toward her, eyes bright with tension. "Why did he stay, and where is Rhyslin?" She tried to keep her tone measured, but a tremor of fear edged her words.

Ixa flicked a cascade of auburn hair over her shoulder and smirked, her eyes catching the firelight like polished amber. "Andros stayed to cover Rhyslin's escape, and now he is leading the creature on a chase through the planes."

Ria's shoulders sagged, relief softening her features. "Rhyslin is okay?" When the elemental nodded, she let out a long, shaky breath. "What do you mean he's leading the creature on a chase?"

Ixa crossed her arms and closed her eyes, her tone lilting with mischief. "Andros covered the creature in an earthen shell, distracting him while Rhyslin got away. Then he—" she laughed, a light, musical sound "—he stuck out his tongue and dared the creature to catch him. So far, he's led the monster through the planes of earth, iron, mud, and magma. He seems to be enjoying himself."

A faint smile ghosted across Ria's lips, but her eyes betrayed the worry she could not silence.
[Oh, Rhyslin, where are you?]

Flur winced and pressed a hand to her temple. Ria turned to her instantly. "What's wrong?"

The Ciad-Bhanna waved her off, forcing a small grin. "It's nothing. I think we all heard you through the bond."

"Oh, I'm sorry," Ria whispered, her voice cracking as guilt and fear tangled within her. "I'm just worried about him."

The fire popped, and another log collapsed inward, sending a brief burst of sparks into the smoky air. Then—

"It's okay, *Mo te Alainn*," came a familiar voice, warm and tired.

Rhyslin stepped through the doorway, framed in the golden light. His cloak was torn at the hem, streaked with soot and something darker, but his eyes were calm and kind.

"I'm here now."

He barely had time to brace himself before Ria collided with him, her arms locking around his chest. He held her close, the tension draining from his face as he pressed his cheek against her hair.

"I didn't mean to worry you," he murmured into her ear.

"I was so worried about you," she whispered into his chest. Slowly, she lifted her gaze, finding her love reflected in his tired smile.

"I thought Flur would be the first into my arms," he teased lightly.

Ria blinked in surprise, halfway between laughter and indignation, only to be saved from answering when Flur leaned in and kissed him. "I knew you'd be okay," she said, affection echoing through their shared bond. "Ria's an old worrywart."

"I am not," Ria replied, trying for composure. "A woman should be worried about her man." Rhyslin squeezed her hand in silent amusement.

"Aww. All this worry for the old *Draoidh* but not a word about the brave elemental that covered his escape."

Andros emerged from the floor in a shimmer of motes, feigning wounded pride.

Rhyslin turned toward him with a grateful grin. "Thank you for the cover, Andros."

The elemental waved him off with a mock flourish. "It was my pleasure. I made him chase me through four planes before he lost me." His grin widened. "I finally lost him on the plane of light."

"Good job," Marcus said, clapping Andros on the back. "You did good." The elemental's laugh boomed like distant thunder, proud and pleased.

The ranger rubbed at the stubble on his chin. "What was that thing? I've never seen anything like it."

"I don't know," Rhyslin admitted, his tone grave. "It is some sort of intelligent shadow creature, and it can either control or block *draoidheacd*." After kissing Flur and hugging Rowena and Rana, he looked about the room, counting familiar faces. "Do we know if Makar, Sloan, and Silas are okay? I hope they didn't have to face that."

"They are upstairs," Marcus replied, nodding toward the ceiling. "They're smarter than we are. They came here at the first sign of trouble and waited for us to show up." He gave a short, tired laugh. "For some reason, that thing didn't try to go after Allanagh or Mayana."

"That might be because it had a bigger group of women to go after," Rhyslin said, accepting a mug of water from the serving maid. He nodded to her with quiet gratitude. "It can't be a coincidence that the first people it tried to attack were our women." He took a long drink, his throat working. "It might be that it feeds on fear."

"That doesn't make sense," Rana said suddenly, breaking her silence. "It kept going on about suffering, how it would make us suffer, how we would suffer."

"Suffering does last longer than fear," Rembran said thoughtfully. "Wounded people suffer days and weeks until wounds heal. Older people suffer pain and infirmity for years. Parents and loved ones suffer long after a loved one dies. Some never recover."

"That's diabolical," Rhyslin muttered. His voice dropped to a growl. "It's a being that feeds upon a universal constant. With enough suffering, nobody could stop it." He frowned, his features tightening as the firelight danced across them. "What god could have created it, and why haven't we seen one until now?"

The question hung heavy in the smoky air. Outside, the wind moaned against the shutters, and somewhere in the distance, thunder rolled, a low, lingering growl, as though the heavens themselves had heard and offered no answer.

Let's Keep in Touch (and in Tales)

Dear Reader,

Thank you for coming along on our third Draoidh's Cearcall adventure. I hope you are enjoying your time in Crann Na Beatha, and that you will return with us for the journeys yet to come.

If you wish to continue these tales, you will find the other stories listed below.

The Draoidh's Cearcall (Series)
1 — *The Draoidh's Cearcall*
2 — *The Draoidh's Gambit*
3 — *The Draoidh's Accord*

Forthcoming
4 — *The Shadows Rise*
5 — *The Draoidh's Fall*

The Law Keeper Chronicles (Series)
1 — *The Black Swan's Bond*

Forthcoming
2 — *The Sheriff's Oath*
3 — *By Law and Flame*

The Web-Weaver's War (Series)
Forthcoming
1 — *Oath & Ember*

If you would like to walk these roads with me as the stories unfold, you are welcome to join my mailing list and author page here:

https://josephwiess.substack.com
https://joseph-l-wiess-author.com

Until next time,
Far þú vel